Whispers in the Woods

Mark Bartholomew

'...xperience with all your senses...the stuff of medieval life'

Kevin Crossley-Holland

Mark Bartholomew

For

Alex, Ethan, Meg and Tony

Acknowledgments:

For their support: Eloise Moore, Chris and Fiona
Furnish, Pete and Jean Moore. The staff at
Stowmarket Middle School and in particular:
Lesley Etchingham, Sheila Johnson, Kathy
Theobald, Kate Kingsford-Bere, Catherine Le
Meur, Helen Kitching, Barry Fuell, Sally Oakes
and Gordon Ewing. Kevin Crossley-Holland for his
advice and guidance. John Lucas, William Oakes,
Sarah Webber, Philip Daws from Ottakar's, and to
the team at Educational Printing Services Limited
for having faith.

First published
January 2006 in Great Britain by

Educational Printing Services Limited

Albion Mill, Water Street, Great Harwood, Blackburn BB6 7QR
Telephone: (01254) 882080   Fax: (01254) 882010
E-mail: enquiries@eprint.co.uk   Website: www.eprint.co.uk

ISBN 1-904904-61-0

'In the forests are the secret places of the King'

(Ralph Fitznigel , 12th Century)

Contents

Throughout many of England's ancient churches strange images appear in amongst the carvings of gargoyles, saints and biblical creatures. These curious faces are often hidden behind branches and leaves. Many people call them green men, some believe them to be visions of nature, some think they are evil . . . but there are other stories about them too.

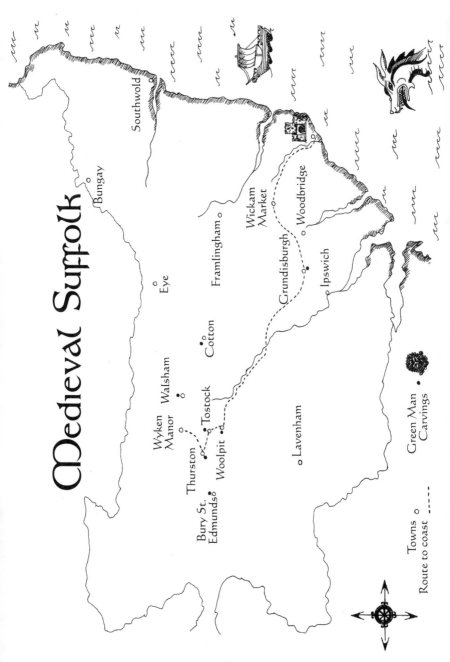

Medieval Suffolk

Southwold

Bungay

Eye

Framlingham

Walsham

Cotton

Wickam Market

Woodbridge

Grundisburgh

Ipswich

Wyken Manor

Tostock

Thurston

Woolpit

Bury St. Edmunds

Lavenham

Green Man Carvings

Towns o

Route to coast - - - - -

2

1: The Finding
~ *The oak tree is the Lord of the Wood* ~

A hazy mist drifted lazily across the wide Suffolk skyline and encircled the village of Woolpit with a ghostly embrace. It wrapped itself tightly around the small settlement and then drifted on upwards to the ancient woodlands, which stood behind the Wolf Pits, silent and secret.

From the last cottage at the south end of the village two figures silently appeared and made their way noiselessly up towards the woods. Morning dew darkened the toes of their leather boots as they strode through the long grasses of the meadow. At the edge of the trees they unslung hunting bows from their shoulders, peered into the undergrowth and disappeared into the shadows.

❦

"Can you see anything yet?" A single eye searched out from the scarred face and stared carefully into the open glade.

"Nothing, this mist is too thick," a deep, throaty voice replied through the clamouring silence of the shady grove.

"Wait, what's that?" The two hunters both

stared at the foot of a vast oak tree.

"There's something moving, make ready with your bow, Cob Fletcher."

At the gnarled roots of the huge, old oak were two small piles of leaves and from underneath one of them, there was movement. Slowly, very slowly, a forest creature was awakening from its sleep and as it moved, the leaves fell to the floor of the wood. Fletcher gently raised his hand to take an arrow from the quiver on his back. He licked its goose feathers, positioned the shaft, drew back the drawstring and took aim.

Then, from underneath the leaves, the creature began to appear, but it was not the foreleg of a deer, or even the white tail of a rabbit that emerged, instead it seemed to be part of the tree itself that moved. "Do you see it?" Fletcher whispered and the other hunter nodded, as his jaw dropped in wonder. It was impossible, but the branch seemed to be alive!

The hunters stared in silence as the green limb pushed through the pile of leaves and then their eyes widened as the branch slowly became an arm. Green fingers sprouted from its tips, they stretched out slowly and then curled back, a shoulder appeared and a back arched upward and then, a green face peered out.

Terrified, Cob Fletcher loosened his fingers

and let fly his arrow and the shaft sped straight towards the beast, but a great branch of the oak tree that towered above them all, swung down suddenly like the brawny arm of a mighty warrior, and knocked the speeding arrow harmlessly to the ground.

The two huntsmen stood rooted to the floor, watching in amazement, as before their eyes a green girl appeared before them. Long, pale hair, the colour of the moon, shook down upon her shoulders and as she moved her emerald dress shimmered in the dappled sunlight.

Turning around, without noticing the men concealed in the trees, the green girl gently brushed the leaves off the remaining pile. Underneath, was a boy, a little younger than her but just as green, with the same pale, ashen hair. Tenderly, she bent down to wake him, wiped a lingering leaf from his face and helped him to his feet.

In the undergrowth, the huntsmen stared at each other with searching eyes. What were they to do now? But they had no time to think; the children already knew someone was watching them. Realising they might run away, Fletcher put aside his fear and moved out from his hiding place but his hunting companion, Tam One-Eye, turned away in terror, stumbled through the bushes and hurtled back to the safety of the village!

"Do not be afraid," the words tumbled awkwardly from Fletcher's mouth as the green children looked fearfully upon him, as he emerged from the trees. It was clear that they did not understand him, for in their eyes they saw only a large man with a hunting bow in his hands. They drew close together, the girl wrapping her arms about the boy like a human shield, and they backed slowly away from him.

"I mean you no harm," he assured them. He spoke quietly now, drawing the children in to him. "Who are you?" he whispered gently.

Moving forward sheepishly, the girl opened her mouth to answer him. As she did so, the huntsman stood in disbelief, as he listened intently to a voice, which was unlike anything he had ever heard before. No real words came from the girl's lips, instead, her voice sang out with wild birdsong. It was a sweet, beautiful, joyous sound but Fletcher didn't understand any of it.

So he tried to make her comprehend again, this time he used his hands to help him. "My name is Cob Fletcher," he pointed to himself in a clumsy manner trying to emphasise what he was saying and then something flickered across the girl's face, some sign of comprehension, a moment of understanding perhaps and she opened her mouth again.

This time the birdsong had fluttered away

7

and in its place a delicate, human voice timidly whispered the words "Clyssa," and pointing at the boy, "Hylasses". To Cob's ears it was a strange tongue, but he assumed that the girl was giving him their names in return.

All of a sudden, without any warning, the green boy swooned and fell to the floor of the glade in a crumpled heap. The girl turned to see her brother collapse and gave out an instinctive cry of despair as Fletcher ran to their aid. As he bent down to help, the girl gripped his wrist and looked him in the eye searchingly. Cob was transfixed; her gaze drew him in, peered into his soul with its intensity. Then, she looked back to the boy and the spell was broken. She released her grip and let Cob pick him up in his arms.

As he rose to leave the woods, however, the green girl seemed to be wary of abandoning the safety of the trees and they in turn were reluctant to let the children leave their care. All around him the oaks and sycamores thrust out their huge, twisting branches to prevent the hunter from passing through.

The girl's anguished look stopped Cob in his tracks but then she gave way to her tiredness and leant despairingly against his firm shoulder. With a face of reassurance he held her close to him and at that sign the trees seemed to relinquish their hold upon the children. Cob pushed his way through the retreating branches, led the green children out from the mists of the woods, past the dark hollows of the Wolf Pits and down into the village.

2: Woolpit

~ In Summer if the sky is blue, the harvest will be good and true ~

The golden sun had risen high into the morning sky and the early morning mists had slipped away like phantoms by the time Cob Fletcher and his strange foundlings had entered the village. Already, a small crowd was gathered around them and as more villagers came off the surrounding fields to see what all the excitement was about, scythes, rakes, and haywains were left behind in the narrow strips of corn, beans and barley that surrounded the humble settlement.

"What have you caught there then, Cob Fletcher? Don't look much like wild coney to me!" a deep voice echoed from the fields.

"Ain't deer either, unless the meat's gone all rotten and turned green," another voice cried from the gathering throng of villagers.

Although they poked fun at the strangers no malice could be heard in their merry voices for the bumper harvest that was now being taken from the fields had raised their spirits. Even so, the expression on the girl's face showed terror as she looked at the crowd around her and as the villagers pushed closer in towards them she tried in vain to disappear behind Cob's cloak. Hard against his arms he could feel her heart beating fast like a captured sparrow.

Cob pushed on but abruptly halted in the centre of the village when he heard a sly voice at the back of the crowd hiss through the amiable atmosphere. It was a child's voice, barely perceptible above the noise of the adults and as he spoke the villagers grew silent and all eyes turned away from the green children and looked upon the boy. He was well dressed in a blue tunic with the device of a silver ship prominent on his chest. He stood with his arms folded and looked around scornfully whilst a liveried servant held two horses by the reins in close attendance.

"They look evil to me!" he exclaimed in disgust. His voice spat out the words with snake-like venom and a solemn hush descended over the throng as he spoke. Then he slipped a boot into his stirrup, pushed himself up and slid a leg over his saddle. "I will inform my father immediately," he declared. He raised his whip to his mount and sped off on his small grey colt, the scurrying servant following in his wake.

"Damn him!" Cob cursed under his breath for he had recognised the boy's voice straight away. It belonged to Simeon de Calne, heir to the Lord of the Manor.

Attention quickly turned back to the green

children. Cob turned to face the questioning crowd and a hush descended as his voice echoed through the street, "These children are indeed strange and as yet have said nothing I really understand. They are frightened, confused and exhausted and all your questions will have to wait, for now. Trust me . . . I am just as curious as all of you."

"What will you do with 'em?" shouted Gan Weaver the swineherd.

"For now I will take them home to Martha and let them rest and take some food and drink if they will," Cob replied and paused for thought, "and then we will just have to wait and see!"

The crowd parted and he carried on walking along the one street of the village, past the ramshackle cottages and the pond and the green until at last he stood at the southern edge of the village. He pushed open the door of the long, thatched house and walked inside still carrying the boy, with the girl, hunched half asleep, under his arm.

As he entered he called softly to his wife, "Martha, come see what I've got here!"

3: The Twins

~ Food and laughter are the best of friends ~

When the green girl finally opened her eyes many hours later, a red sun had already begun to descend. Outside, the villagers were finishing their labours in the fields and tiredly returning to their homes, but inside the Fletcher's cottage, she looked around her new surroundings with wonder.

She was in the corner of a long, dim room. Above her was not a canopy of trees but a roof made of thatched reeds. There were some wooden chairs and a table huddled around a great open fire in the centre of the room and over it a pot stood on an iron frame and bubbled and boiled away soothingly.

There were two small windows set on either side of the building and through them a thin beam of light lit the floor, which was covered in freshly cut reeds. A warm breeze filtered in, for there was no glass in the windows and this fanned the fire. A woody smoke funnelled towards the openings for there was no chimney either. It was a humble, yet cosy dwelling, and there was a pleasant atmosphere here, she could feel that, though she could not explain why.

Then, she noticed two children at the far end

of the room busily labouring away in the light of the doorway. They appeared to be weaving willow stems to make a large basket. They laughed and giggled merrily as they worked and their sound warmed the cottage as well as the girl's heart and she reached over and gently put a hand on her brother's shoulder as he continued his slumber.

As she turned back to the children, a woman walked into the cottage carrying a large basket of vegetables, she crossed to the fire and sat down. She spoke gently but firmly to the children and they settled back down to their task whilst she picked up a small bone-handled knife and started to peel the carrots and strip the peas.

Suddenly, the girl's belly groaned with emptiness and she tried to recall when she had last eaten but it was no use, she could remember no further back than when the man with the kind eyes had found them in the woods. So, she lay her head back down on the warm straw bed and as dark shadows flickered across her mind again she fell instantly back into a fitful sleep.

❧

The sun had finally fallen, day had ended and the village of Woolpit now lay wrapped in a dark blanket of night. Cob and Martha Fletcher had already taken to their bed but elsewhere in the cottage two small figures were still awake.

Slowly and carefully the Fletcher twins worked their way out of their bed without making a sound. They tiptoed past their parents, neatly hopped over the sleeping dog laid out in front of the dying fire and crawled over to where the two green children lay huddled under a blanket.

The green children were sleeping soundly but as the twins drew closer and peered down upon them with starry-eyed wonder, something stirred them and suddenly they awoke and gazed up into the enquiring eyes of the Fletcher children. The twins fell back in surprise, "Father!" shouted the boy, "They is awake!"

Cob Fletcher grunted sleepily from across the other side of the room and clambered out of bed. He wrapped himself in a woollen blanket, stumbled past the dozing dog and came to greet his visitors. Moments later Martha Fletcher joined him.

"Did you wake them, Till Fletcher?" she glared at the lad.

"No Mother," said the boy indignantly.

"Wasn't me either!" said his twin sister.

"Are you sure, Meg?"

"No Mother, honest," pleaded the young girl.

"They did not wake us," the green girl spoke in their defence.

The Fletchers looked upon her in

astonishment. "I thought you said they couldn't speak?" Martha stared at Cob, bemused.

"I said I couldn't understand them," her husband replied. "Where are you from?" Cob asked softly as he knelt down next to the girl.

"The trees I think," she replied hesitantly.

"Where are your family?"

"I don't remember."

"How did you come to be in the woods?" Cob continued to probe.

"I don't remember," the green girl repeated the words slowly and her eyes filled with tears. Images blinked through her mind like captured glances in a broken mirror. She saw a green face like her own, but bearded, she saw clear, grey eyes like her brother's and a smile that reflected back out of the gloomy corners of her dark memory. And then the face was gone!

Cob turned to the boy but he too seemed lost and confused and as his questions bounced off the green children's memories, like arrows against a castle wall, it was clear to all that something terrible had happened to these two strange children.

"What do you remember then?" Cob finally asked, exasperated.

"I remember very little," stated the girl woefully, "my father's face, cries of anger and heavy footsteps, then nothing. It's as if my memory has been stolen from me." She wept sadly and the Fletchers looked on helplessly.

"Well it's late, and we all need some rest." Cob's voice was soothing, calm, and fatherly. "We will talk again in the morning." He cajoled the twins back to their beds whilst Martha tucked the green children back into theirs. She stroked their faces and sat by them until they closed their eyes again. She watched over them for a few brief moments and when she was assured that they had settled she tip-toed back to her own bed.

4: The Healing Stones

~ Roots, trees, leaves and flowers; all of these
have healing powers~

By the following morning, a small crowd was already waiting expectantly outside the Fletcher's door, intent on catching a glimpse of the strangers or at the very least hearing news from Cob as to who they were.

Inside the cottage, the two guests were eating a breakfast of porridge timidly, for the food was very strange to them. Then, fed up with the noise outside, Cob wiped his chin and crossed the room to the front door. As he stuck his head out, a silence fell swiftly over the gathering. "Right you lot," he stated loudly, "I will say this once and only once! It would appear that these children, for that is what they are, have lost their father, they live in the woods and something terrible seems to have happened. Their memories of almost everything are lost too. They can speak a few words and they appear to be learning more every minute. They will be staying with us for now but as for the future I don't rightly know." Cob took a breath, "They will, I am sure, come out when they are good and ready but for now you can all go about your business. It's harvest time after all and no one, and that includes you Tam One-Eye, should be standing around here idling the day away. Good-day!" And with that he shut the door again before anyone in the crowd could utter a single word, let alone ask a question.

The villagers looked about each other dumbstruck. The torrent of words from Cob had left them in somewhat of a shock and they did indeed realise that that was it for now. Within minutes they had gone their separate ways into the fields and left the Fletchers and their curious guests to themselves.

By late morning the two green children were good and ready to go outside. Till and Meg had offered to show them around the village whilst Cob and Martha went out to help with the harvest and the twins couldn't believe their luck when their father had agreed; they whooped with delight at being let off the back-breaking work.

"Don't get into any mischief and be back here by suppertime," Cob ordered.

"Yes Father," the twins spoke in unison.

When they left the cottage, Martha handed Meg a willow basket with some food inside, smiled down upon her green guests and wiped a lump of cold porridge from Till's face with her apron.

Once outside the twins took the green children by the hand and led them along the village street pointing at the villeins' cottages and reeling off the names of all the people that lived in them. There were far too many for the green children to remember and the strange language was still harsh and unfamiliar to their ears so Till and Meg had to speak very slowly and repeat things a number of times over so they could understand.

They ran across the common land, where the sheep and the thin cattle were grazing and as they passed the church the green children stared in amazement at the stone building of St. Mary's. Then, they rushed past the staring eyes of the men and the women in the field. Corn was slowly falling under their swinging scythes, narrow strips of vegetables were slowly uprooted and fruit was carefully picked as Woolpit's harvest was brought home.

Whilst the warm summer sun smiled down upon them, the children carefully climbed the small hill that rose gently to the east of the village and sat down upon the grass to survey the scene before them. To the twins' eyes it was a common enough sight; the villagers working on the cultivated land, the golden sun glinting on the great church spire, the oxen and the haywains rolling rhythmically back and forth across the fields like the pendulum of a great clock. But, the green children looked upon things they had never

seen before and though they stared with wonder at what was new, they also felt sadness at what now seemed lost to them.

They both turned to look back to the woods and then spotted something strange.

"What are those?" the green boy asked, as he pointed to a dozen or so stones that were hanging from the trees by pieces of rope.

"Those are healing stones," replied Till.

"What do they do?" the green girl became interested.

"When somebody in your family is ill, you hang a stone from the tree - the illness will soon be cleared for the trees have healing powers," Meg answered.

"Yes, we know," the girl, replied with an air of understanding.

They approached the stones thoughtfully and while the green boy stared at them with intrigue, the green girl put her hand to the trunk of the nearest tree and brushed her outstretched fingers through its leaves as if she was greeting an old friend. She spoke softly, her words barely audible in the breeze and closed her eyes as if in prayer. Meg and Till thought they heard the woods whisper in reply and they stared at the girl in curiosity, but before they could ask her what she was doing a loud clanging reverberated up from the village.

The green children instinctively clamped their hands over their ears and cowered upon the ground, they had never heard such a din. It took the twins a good five minutes before the green children would let them release their hands to explain that it was only the church bells tolling for mid-day.

Once that was made clear, Till decided that it was a suitable time to eat and tugged at the wicker basket that his sister held so tightly. "Come on, I'm starving!" he exclaimed and snatched out the small, round white bread that his mother had made that morning.

"We cannot eat that!" said the green boy as he pointed to the bread.

"Why not?" said Till, as he placed the loaf on the ground before them.

"It's just a stone!" said the boy.

Till laughed, "No it isn't, it's bread," and he proceeded to tear off a great hunk of the loaf and stuff his mouth with it.

"It's made from the wheat," Meg explained, as she sat down next to her brother and took out a cheese. "The wheat is ground down to make a white powder we call flour. Barnet the Miller does it. The flour then makes a dough which is cooked to make the bread. Have some quick before greedy-guts here eats it all," she snatched up the loaf quickly and broke off some of the bread for the children.

"It tastes good!" the green boy smiled as he chewed eagerly on the crust.

This action seemed to open up a flood of questions from the green children. For their part the twins answered all they could. What the church stood for, who the Pope was (though it was clear, Till himself was not entirely sure). They told them about the Lord of the Manor and the King in his castle in the great city of London where it was said the roads were made of gold. They told the children about the faraway battles, which Father called 'crusades', they recounted tales of the sea and the sailing ships that brought trade to the ports. They talked of the animals that they kept, the different crops that were grown, the games they played and the songs they sang. How they learnt their letters (which they rarely did) and how they looked forward to the Summers and dreaded the Winters.

As the shadows lengthened, the afternoon passed gently away in idle talk but in all that time the twins got little back from their guests, for the green children could tell nothing of their woodland world. Their memories, it seemed, were laid as stark and as skeletal as trees in Winter.

By the time the four children returned to the Fletcher's cottage it was almost dusk. They were greeted with a warm supper of mushroom stew and more bread and then Martha softly sang them all to sleep. But the green children's night was not a good one; dark images swam through their dreams, their father's face drifted in and out of their subconscious and their memories drowned in a sea of despair.

5: Camp-ball

~ The strongest horse doesn't always win the race ~

A bright golden sun greeted the children as Meg and Till and their green visitors rushed outside into the morning air of the new day. There was an eager feeling of excitement all around the village that morning. Indeed many of the younger boys had looked forward to this particular date for many weeks now. For today was the great annual event to mark the end of harvest. It was the day the whole village turned out to watch and take part in one of the games Till had raved about just yesterday. Today was the day of the camp-ball game.

Within minutes, all the villagers had spilled out of their cottages and amassed around the centre of Woolpit. Then Cob, Till and around thirty other men and boys gathered together and jostled, shoved and barged each other whilst they waited expectantly in the middle of the common land. Around the edge of the green, the women and those too young or too old or just too wise also waited anxiously for the game to begin.

At the front of the crowd the green boy stood next to his sister as they, and Meg and Martha Fletcher, watched the proceedings eagerly.

27

"Come and join in lad!" Cob shouted to the boy as he jogged to the middle of the green.

"No, Cob, he'll get hurt!" Martha cried out to her husband.

"He'll be fine woman!" Cob retorted back.

The green boy needed no more encouragement; he grinned at his sister and quickly ran over to Fletcher's side.

Even though the sheep and pigs that grazed on the common land were still in the way, the game was about to begin. A tall, stork-like old man with a long beak-like nose walked out from the crowd and brought some order to the proceedings. This was Will Middlefoot, the Reeve, and he held aloft an inflated pig's bladder stuffed with dried peas, which acted as a ball and called the players around him. Meanwhile, Till hurriedly explained the rules to the green boy.

"It's very simple. The team that gets the camp-ball to the opponents' end of the village wins. Our cottage is at the south end so we're the Southers, Tam One-Eye's is at the north end so his team are the Northers. You can't use clubs, knives or cudgels, but you can use your hands, feet - even your backside if you want. Otherwise, there are no rules! Just keep it away from the Northers and especially keep out of the way of that great stinking oaf over there." Till pointed to a hulking lad of about seventeen years of age.

"Bull Weaver," he said, "the swineherd's eldest. Last year, he broke two lads' legs and gave me a black eye that lasted a month. Even Father keeps away from him - so be careful!" Bull Weaver eyed them suspiciously; he wiped sweat from his fat, muddy face, swore at no-one in particular and spat on the grass as if ready to charge.

Suddenly, Old Will threw the camp-ball high, high into the air, the onlookers cheered and the game began. Hands reached upward, fingers outstretched, shoulders barged, elbows dug and feet kicked, in a storm of excited limbs. Till and the green boy quickly realised there was no point in them jumping for they were far too small, so they stood behind the throng of players and awaited the outcome of this initial encounter.

Cob was the first to get his hands on the ball. He caught it skilfully but then fell with a thud to the floor. Before he could get up Tam One-Eye trod on his hand and kicked the loose ball free. A shout went up for 'The Northers' and Tam led a charge toward the escaping ball. It was John Middlefoot, the reeve's son, who collected it for the Northers. In no time at all he ran across the common and headed south. As Middlefoot ran, the game progressed rapidly along the street and a crowd of Southers led by Cob tackled him. In answer, the Northers charged in. A great scrum then ensued pushing

30

first back down to the common and then up toward Cob's cottage - the Southers's goal.

It was brute force and muscle that would win this encounter and the Northers had plenty in their ranks. A noisy heaving, pushing, shoving, kicking and even biting followed and slowly but surely, the Southers were forced into a retreat and now the horde stood just yards from Cob's front door.

Then, from out of the pack Tam One-Eye was forcefully propelled with the ball couched under his left arm. Just as it looked as if he would win the day for the Northers, a last desperate lunge by Cob caught his ankle and pulled him to the ground. The camp-ball, with its dried peas rattling inside, thumped Tam on the head and bounced loose again like a slippery eel.

This time it was Till who picked up the ball. He had virtually the whole length of the village before him but it was a clear run ahead. He shoved the ball under his arm and ran for his life. Everyone followed behind him!

He dodged past Barnet the Miller, slipped through the legs of Aethlus the Hayward, jumped clean over a stray ewe and landed deftly by the fishpond. But then a dark shadow covered Till completely. From nowhere a huge forearm smashed down toward him. It was Bull Weaver! He had laid hidden in wait at the back of the pack as a last line of defence. The blow knocked the ball from Till's grip and sent him flying headlong into the water with a crunching jolt.

The camp-ball bounced hard on the ground and then up towards the outstretched hands of a grinning Bull Weaver. Once he had the ball the Northers were home and dry – no one could tackle him!

But then a small figure darted out from the onrushing herd of players like a speeding arrow, and seconds before Bull had his great paws around the ball he snatched it from him - it was the green boy! A huge cheer went up from the onlookers and Bull Weaver could only stand dumbfounded - his feet anchored to the floor.

"Run!" shouted Till as he pulled himself out of the murky water and removed a small, dazed frog from his undershirt.

The green boy looked behind and saw twenty angry Northers trampling towards him and then he charged for the goaline. His speed was astonishing. No one could catch him! And it seemed to many that watched in awe, that he ran more with the grace and agility of a sprinting deer than that of a young boy.

Bull Weaver looked on helplessly as sweet victory turned to bitter defeat. He stamped up and down like a moody toddler and as Till emerged soaked from the pond, he turned and pushed him back in again, uttering a curse.

But the day belonged to the Southers and as the green boy stood proudly outside the door of Tam One-Eye's cottage, it was they who ran towards him now and lifted him aloft. For the first time since he had been found, the green boy smiled from ear to ear. A beaming Cob broke away from the celebrations and shouted over to Martha, "There woman, I told you he'd come to no harm!"

6: Nuncy

~ *A hot broth is nothing, without herbs* ~

It was almost noon by the time the four children came back into the village. After the rigours of the camp-ball game they had spent much of the morning up by the edge of the wood where the green children had been found. Fruitlessly, they had searched in and out of the hedgerows and thickets trying to find some clue as to the children's origin but eventually, they had given up. As they crossed the newly harvested top field they left sight of the trees and the two green children once again fell into sadness, their faces downcast and mournful.

Then, for the second time that day, the familiar voice of Bull Weaver echoed out an ill-tempered curse. The recipient this time, however, was not a camp-ball player but a large black, muddy sow known locally as 'Jezebel'. As the children glanced down to the bottom of the field they saw Weaver in pursuit of the pig.

"Seems like you've really lost your touch, Bull!" Till shouted to the swineherd's son, as he laughed out loud.

Weaver ignored Till's comments and struggled in vain to throw his rope around Jezebel's fat neck but then, as the lasso fell to no avail upon the ground,

the great sow put her foot in the loop and Bull
thought he had her. Hurriedly, he wrapped his end
of the rope around his left wrist and pulled it
tight.

It was a big mistake! Jezebel had no
intention of being pulled unceremoniously back
into her pen, especially by the leg. She snorted
out loud and stood firm. Bull pulled and swore
and pulled some more but there was no moving
the stubborn pig.

Then, to the everlasting amusement of Till
Fletcher, Jezebel decided that she too would take
part in this Tug-of-War. With all her might she
strode forward. For a moment or two the contest
looked even, Bull was a big lad after all, but in
the end it was Jezebel who took the honours. In
one last great effort the old sow stamped her feet
down and hauled herself forward. Bull was
yanked forcefully out of his boots and headlong
into the mud!

On the far side of the field, Till fell to the
floor in laughter as the other three children looked
on with amusement and a sliver of sympathy for
the swineherd's son.

"He'll catch it now!" exclaimed Meg. "His
father will give him a good beating."

"Serves him right!" remarked Till. "Look at
her go!" Jezebel was off and running. "Watch out
she's coming this way," Meg warned, as she and
Till ran down the hill but the two green children

stood firm.

The girl then walked slowly and calmly toward the grunting sow while it stopped to feast on a clump of large black field mushrooms. For a few brief moments, she seemed to utter words to the great animal and then, very slowly, the pig turned and sauntered back into its pen. Bull quickly picked himself up from the mud, grabbed the wooden gate and shut it tightly behind her. He looked up to the green girl in astonishment but found no words to say. Instead, he nodded his head in thanks and turned away to make sure the Weaver family's prize possession got a good telling off.

The green girl smiled and with a lighter step, she and her brother ran down to the twins.

"How did you do that?" Meg asked in amazement.

"I just asked her to go home," the girl answered.

"Yeah, sure you did!" Till exclaimed. "Come on let's go, all that laughing has made me hungry," and off they sped, down into the village.

As the children entered the Fletcher cottage and swarmed around the fireside, they noticed someone sleeping comfortably in the chair by the hearth. A gentle snoring like the purr of an old cat drifted forth from the figure and as they gathered around the twins recognised the visitor immediately.

"Who is that?" the green girl asked tentatively.

"That's Nunty, our grandmother," the twins answered in unison.

"You were found in Nunty's Wood," Till stated proudly.

"She used to take us there and teach us the names of the trees and flowers and birds. But now she cannot make any sense with her words at all, they fall from her lips like rain and splatter on the floor in garbled puddles," Meg lamented and as she turned away, a single tear slipped down her cheek and glistened like morning dew in the light of the fire.

Then, as if she knew she was being talked about the wizened old figure sparked into life. She babbled and chattered nonsense to herself as the children looked on. But when she turned towards them and her gibberish stopped, a smile crossed her lips as she cast her eyes upon the green children. Then, she slipped back once again into that twilight world that lies between sleep and waking, for old age had caught up with Nunty and soon the long night would be upon her.

Suddenly, the green girl crossed the floor of

the cottage and knelt down by the old woman.
She clasped her wrinkled, old hand tightly and
looked deep into her eyes, for a moment she held
her gaze and then she rose again and turned to
the twins.

"Do you have any moridias?" she asked them.

"I don't even know what it is," replied Till,
"so how would I know if we had any?"

Meg too, looked bewildered.

"It's a plant. It grows in the woods," she
replied earnestly and headed to the door of the
cottage. "Come on!" she cried. "Let's see if we
can find some."

"But why?" asked Till.

"So we can help her of course!" the girl
answered him, as she pointed to Nunty.

Till and Meg looked at each other utterly
bemused but they followed the girl instinctively
and all four of the children headed outside and
back up to the woods.

꧁꧂

Barely a quarter of an hour later the green girl
called the others around her as she triumphantly
pulled up a handful of leaves from a spiky, green
plant. "At last, I've found some," she gasped.

"But that's just Jack-by-the hedge," Till
looked baffled. "Mother puts that in the stew, I
hate it!"

"Well, it's very useful," the girl answered, "but I need something to go with it."

She looked carefully along the edge of the wood and through the hedgerows. Her eyes passed over patches of woodruff, wild thyme and goosegrass and then she saw what she was after. In the shadow of a large beech tree she bent down and gently took a handful of shamrock shaped leaves from a young wood sorrel plant.

"We call this 'askantha'," she said, "that I do remember and it means life-giver."

"We call it sour sally," Till screwed up his face, "and I don't like that much either!"

"Yes, but it is also known as fairybells," remarked Meg as if to support the green girl's positive view of the wood sorrel.

"Have you everything you need?" she asked.

"Yes," the green girl smiled.

"Let's go home then," Till stated. "My stomach's rumbling."

"Oh, I thought that was thunder," Meg teased him.

"Very funny!" Till shouted, as he ran for home.

As Till hung expectantly around his mother's skirts waiting for food, the green girl carefully crushed her leaves with a pestle and mortar before

39

dropping them into a small cauldron of boiling water. Within moments a pale green steam arose from the iron pot and the girl chanted a soft, melodious song over the simmering mixture. Then, she poured the draft into an earthenware bowl and blew gently upon it to cool it down.

The concoction smelt sweet and pleasant, its aroma drifted right through the cottage and everyone gathered around as the girl passed the bowl to Meg who in turn took it across to Nunty, who still sat mumbling by the fireside.
She put the old woman's wizened old fingers tightly round the bowl and then she helped her raise it to her lips. Nunty drank quickly and noisily and finished the bowl with a satisfied smile. Then she sat back down in her chair as the others edged closer.

For a moment, nothing happened, but then a pale green light seemed to shine in the old woman's face. Her eyes appeared to twinkle in the gloom of the cottage and the tight lines of age that hung heavily around her mouth loosened. Suddenly, to the wonder of everyone, she rose to her feet and stood as firm and as strong as a young sapling.

Cob and Martha crossed the room from where they were peeling vegetables and watched in astonishment. Then Nunty turned to her son, smiled at him and spoke, "When do we eat

Cob?" she asked with a grin. "You always were slow to put supper on the table!"

It was the first time in nearly a year that she had spoken anything other than a jumble of meaningless words. Cob was so astounded he dropped his bowl of half-peeled carrots and they splattered across the floor. He stood quite still, his mouth open like a dead fish, and then he laughed out loud, drew the old woman into his arms and held his mother close to him.

Martha sat down heavily upon a stool, stared at the green girl and gasped out loud, "How have you done this? Is it magic?"

"No," the girl replied calmly. "It is knowledge. It's something I don't need to remember, it's deep down inside of me."

"Whatever it is, it's marvellous," Meg shouted excitedly and she ran over to the green girl and wrapped her arms around her in gratitude. She had her grandmother back!

After supper, as the family and their new friends sat quietly down upon the reed floor, Cob put a gentle hand on the green girl's shoulders and looked deep into her eyes. "Thank you," he said, "thank you, for what you have done. I will not forget this."

For the next few hours, they sat by the fire and listened intently as Nunty once again entertained everyone with the tall tales of her father. Old Tom had been a fisherman on the Suffolk coast and she told of how he had once been swallowed whole by a great whale and was only spat out when he lit a fire inside its belly. She recounted how he had been captured by wicked French pirates and how he used to race his boat against swarms of flying fish and though Till and Meg and Cob and Martha had heard them all many times before, they sat in hushed awe before the old woman's feet.

7: The Loaf-Mass

~ *Cut your own bread and you'll never go hungry* ~

A mild breeze swept across the fields like the warm breath of some great giant. And under the cloudless, crimson sky the dying sun cast long shadows on the red earth as a large crowd of villagers gathered in the top field.

A number of men moved forward from the gathering in a slow, deliberate manner. They walked out into the middle of the field and started to go to work. A yoke was laid upon the oxen's shoulders and then attached to a plough. Will Middlefoot, the Reeve, came forward and took the handle of the plough beam. He lowered it gently to the soil and shouted a command to the oxen.

Slowly, ponderously they trudged forward along the narrow strip of land. The coulter blade cut into the ground, the plough share sliced through the red, Suffolk clay and behind it the mould board turned the soil over. Within a few minutes a deep new furrow lay in the red earth and a happy cheer rose from the congregation of on-looking villagers.

Then from the front of the gathering the thin, gangly figure of the priest moved out. Solemnly and silently Brother Cuthbert, carrying a small bundle, walked over to the freshly ploughed furrow. He carefully undid it and took out a loaf of bread. For this was the Lammas, the loaf-mass, made with the first flour from this year's harvest and ceremoniously he laid it in the furrow and covered it with earth.

He spoke in prayer and the villagers bowed their heads in due reverence. "Thank you Lord for the harvest you have given us and for the sun and rain that gave life to our crops." Silently, the crowd in turn gave their thanks to God and then quietly turned away from the top field.

"Now for some real thanksgiving," roared Tam One-Eye and a joyful cheer echoed throughout the village. The religious ceremony was over and now the real festivities would begin and tonight under the trees a far older, pagan thanksgiving would be held.

ᚌᚌᚌ

Each year, when summer was at its kindest and when the harvest had been gathered to make the long grey months of the winter more bearable, the people of Woolpit celebrated with a great feast.

Under a canopy of trees, by the edge of Nunty's wood, on the rise just above the settlement, the villagers scurried this way and that way like ants, carrying, fetching, loading and unloading in preparation for the spread. From up here the villagers could look down proudly upon their homes and their harvested lands and enjoy a well-earned treat after long, hard months of back-breaking ploughing, sowing, weeding, hoeing and threshing.

So as the final trestle tables and benches arrived from the Manor house, on a great cart pulled by two fat oxen and as the sun slipped away and the stars came out to dance in the darkening sky above, torches were lit and a great bonfire was set alight. It was not long before laughter resonated through the cathedral of boughs and music and song reverberated out across the fields and surrounding woodlands.

The two green children were there and they sat between Till and Meg and stared at the festivities around them with a mixture of wonder and bewildered excitement. Their hungry eyes devoured the joyful scene around them whilst their ears gulped in the laughter. Nearby, Cob chatted merrily with Tam One-Eye whilst Martha passed up and down the tables ensuring everyone had what they wanted and beside them the Fletcher twins giggled and scoffed away hungrily. They knew times like this were few and

far between and they had learnt how to make the most of such celebrations.

"It's a B!" Till laughed out loudly.

He had just watched his sister carefully peel a bright red apple and then drop the peel on the grass. Then he had jumped off the bench, burped loudly, and crouched down slowly to study the peel very carefully. He had then let out his great belly laugh. "I can't believe it, Meggy, it's a B!" and he fell about in delight.

"Why does he laugh so?" asked the green girl.

"Well," said Meg, with a look of scorn, "some people say that you can tell the initial of who you are going to marry by looking at the letter formed by the peel."

"Yes and it's a B," repeated Till again, as he continued to chuckle. "That means only one person . . . Bull Weaver!" He laughed again, tripped on his bench, knocked his plate all over himself and crashed back down to the floor.

"Serves you right!" said Meg, "and besides, it could mean anyone. Who knows who I might meet some day, some brave knight or baron perhaps?"

"Or a pig herder's son," Till stated merrily as he removed a white splodge of egg from his forehead.

The green children joined in the eating and

hungrily devoured the cheese and the apples and the bread. They filled their platters with nuts and berries and spiced plums but would not allow any meat to pass their lips.

Then, as the green girl reached across to sip her mug of water something caught her eye and she turned to Meg with a look of horror, "Why does your father drink blood?" she gasped.

"He does not!" Meg replied indignantly.

"Then what is that being poured into his cup?" she continued.

Meg laughed. "That's wine!" she exclaimed. "It's crushed berries. It's very strong and if he drinks too much it makes him loud and silly in the evening and very grumpy in the morning."

At that moment, Tam One-Eye, who had clearly drunk too much 'blood' already, toppled off his bench and landed with a thud upon the grass. Cob helped him to his feet and walked him over to the nearest tree. For the remainder of the evening he lay happily slumped against its trunk with a huge grin upon his round, scarred face.

"Tam is my Godsib," said Till, as the children watched him in amusement. "He gave me my name."

"And mine," interrupted Meg .

"He named me Till because he hopes I will be a great farmer and till the soil well."

"And I'm Meg because his wife was called

that and he said she was as pretty as me when I was born."

"Yes, but now look at you!" sneered Till.

"What happened to his wife?" the green boy asked.

"She died from the fever," Meg stated.

"What is fever?" asked the girl.

"A disease, an illness. You become all hot and sweaty and you cannot eat and eventually you just fade away."

"Have you no viriditas?"

It was Meg's turn to be confused now. "What is that?" she asked back.

"I think you would call it medicine."

"We have some cures but they rarely work," Meg stated.

The green girl smiled as if pleased she could at last do something in return for the kindness she and her brother had been shown. "Then perhaps we can help you," she replied.

"Why does he only have one eye?" the green boy looked across to the tree where Tam was now snoring loudly.

"When he was young he was caught poaching on the Abbot's land and that was his punishment." The green children looked at each other in alarm and shuddered at the cruelty of their hosts. "Still he was lucky it was not even worse," Till continued. "His Lordship stopped the sentence in time to save his sight, the Abbot wanted both eyes!"

As the villagers filled up their bellies and as the wine began to take effect, a number of the men picked up their musical instruments and began to play. At first, the two green children jumped with alarm as this makeshift band with their strange looking instruments struck up a tune.

Aethlus the Hayward blew hard upon the bagpipes, so hard in fact his face turned bright purple. Gan the Swineherd fiddled lightly on the rebec, no mean feat for a man of his girth. Barnet the Miller bashed enthusiastically upon the tabor drum and Cob himself played the shawm. The noise, for there was little melody, terrified the green children, who clasped their hands tightly over their ears but eventually the players found a more harmonious tune and the children grew used to the din.

By this time a number of villagers were already up and dancing, including the twins. They threw each other round and round in a merry jig and then to the amusement of all, Bull Weaver bowed in front of the dancers and joined in their circle. At the point where Bull took Meg's hand, Till had an attack of the giggles, missed his own turn and had to leave the dance. Meg's face blushed and the green children grinned.

Finally, when the dancing had come to an end, old Will Middlefoot rose to speak to the happy throng. He lifted his old frame up onto the top table and stood, much to the entertainment of the crowd, with his face in the leaves. He pushed a branch out of his way and addressed the crowd.

"Well my friends, we have gathered our harvest and a grand one it is too. Michaelmas will be a might easier now and many of us can live comfortably right through to Candlemas," he stated proudly amidst a great cheer. "And if it was God's will that we have raised such a healthy crop," he continued, "I'm certain that the arrival of our green friends here has also proved a good omen." At that point all eyes turned to the children who blushed under the gaze, at least as far as it was possible for green skin to turn red.

"Now for some singing," Will shouted, "who will start us off?" Within seconds Gan Weaver and Barnet the Miller arose upon ale-weary legs and started to drone out a familiar old harvesting song to the gathering.

John Barleycorn

"They ploughed in the earth so deep,
threw clods all over his head.
They made a vow, a solemn vow,
John Barleycorn was dead,
John Barleycorn was dead.

They hired men with pitchforks stout;
they cut him through the heart,
and after they had served him so,
they tied him to a cart, they tied him to a cart ."

After a pleasing round of applause, Old
Will himself stood up to offer his own song. As
he sang he danced and jigged upon the table top
and the crowd around him clapped and sang
along.

The Old Grey Mare

"Now, I'm an old country Reeve,
no nobleman am I.
I whistle and sing from morn to night,
and trouble I'll defy.
I've one to bear my company;
of work she does her share.
It's not my wife, upon my life,
but a rattling old grey mare.

It's up and down the village track
my mare and I we go.
The folks all kindly greet us
as we journey to and fro.
The little ones they shout hello
and the old just stop and stare,
And lift their eyes with great surprise
at Will and his old grey mare.

Now I would not change my station
with the noblest in the land,
I would not be King or anything so grand.
I would not be a nobleman to live in luxury,
If it would separate, the old grey mare and me."

When he had finished, he bowed grandly and stepped down to a multitude of resounding cheers. And once he had caught his breath and taken a sip of ale, he brought the company to silence and turned to the green children.

"Well you have heard our tunes, now perhaps you can remember one of your songs and share it with us?" he asked. Once again, the villagers all turned their attention to the children and waited expectantly for an answer. Then the girl rose up and walked over to where Old Will was standing. She stood next to him, straight and proud, but her voice trembled as she spoke.

"There is only one song I can recall, it seems as if it were just yesterday that I heard it. I will sing it for you, but I can only perform it in our tongue." As she began to sing the green boy sat down next to the twins and started to whisper a translation in their ears.

The Lay of the Green King

The Lord of all the Greenwood,
the Guardian of the trees.
The King of Golden Summer, now runs
and hides and flees.

The green forest is his home,
But his Kingdom now is dying.
There no longer does he roam,
in ruin, it is lying.

The Lord of all the Greenwood,
the Guardian of the trees.
The King of Golden Summer, now runs
and hides, and flees.

Lonely, the birds call out his name,
the owls cry in the night.
Softly, the woods whisper the blame
But, will he return to fight?

The Lord of all the Greenwood,
the Guardian of the trees.
The King of Golden Summer, now runs
and hides, and flees.

Yet, his power can still be found,
behind every branch and leaf.
A green King will again be crowned
and save us all from grief.

The Lord of all the Greenwood,
the Guardian of the trees.
Will return once more again to his
Kingdom in the leaves.

The villagers had heard nothing like it
before; it was at once both unworldly and yet
utterly natural. They realised their own singing
now seemed crude in comparison with her
beautiful, sweet voice. A voice so clear and
resonant that all those around stood in absolute
silence, even the trees leant close and bent their
ears to the wonderful melody. As she sang, only
tears accompanied her and when she had finished
her mournful song her brother rose from his seat,
ran to her, and pulled her close.

Then, as if their troubles had come rushing
back to them, they slumped to the floor. A heavy
tiredness flooded over them like the ocean's
waves. The villagers rose together as one and
picked their strange visitors up and the two slight
figures were brought to rest under the trees. They
drifted off to sleep with the sounds of soft
laughter and merrymaking in their ears and after

the celebration had ended, when the dark night had come, they were gently carried back to the Fletcher's cottage.

A loud, brash knocking broke through the stillness of the bright morning, nearly shaking the door of the Fletcher's home off its hinges. The two green children awoke with a start. They heard muffled voices on the doorstep and then a loud voice rang through the tiny cottage. "His Lordship will take them now!"

8: Wyken Manor

~ Good counsel comes from good men ~

The surly, liveried servant lifted the heavy bar of the great, oak doors of Wyken Manor and swung them inwards grumbling on their rusty hinges. The two green children took one last, lingering look outside and then left the bright morning behind them as the attendant ushered them reluctantly inside.

They found themselves in a great hall, which was wide and grand and filled with shadows. Great wooden pillars rose from the stone floor as if they were living trees holding up an intricately carved ceiling that lay above them. As their eyes grew accustomed to the dim light the children stared up at the gallery. Here, all along the walls were great shields which dazzled and shimmered in the half-light with heraldic designs. Rampant lions and sleeping dragons peered down upon them from the gloom above. Strange shapes and odd patterns in a myriad of colours bedazzled them. Fleur-de-lys, crescent moons, axes and swords all sparkled on their bright backgrounds. Yet one motif stood out more than any other. Repeated on a number of the shields and mirrored throughout the hall's carvings and wall hangings was that of a silver ship on an azure background; the ancient device of the de Calne family. Standing there in the great hall the two green children once again felt lost, lonely and unwelcome.

The servant quickly rushed them through the hallway, along a narrow passage and then they stopped abruptly before another great oak door. A noisy din came from the room within and the children suddenly felt nervous and afraid but the servant, oblivious to their feelings, opened the door to the Hundred Court and herded them in.

The court was packed full of villagers, who stood chattering and gossiping all around the chamber but as the servant led the green children inside, a hushed silence fell upon everyone present. They walked forward slowly, their heads bent low under the watchful stares of the crowd and as they approached the front of the court someone, unseen, stuck out a leg and the green boy tripped and fell hard upon the cold, stone floor. The outstretched limb was pulled hurriedly back in again as a loud chorus of laughter echoed through the hall and a huge roar in particular rose from a group of boys from where the leg had come.

This nest of vipers giggled and cackled venomously and as the green girl helped her brother to his feet she glared across at them. She recognised one face in particular, and a sly grin stared back coldly at her. It was the boy she had seen in the village that first day; the one who had galloped away - it was Simeon de Calne.

The children were quickly led away to the far side of the room, where they were sat down on a bench to await their hearing in front of the Lord of the Manor. Next to them a studious clerk sat on a stool and wrote hurriedly with his quill pen on some parchment. Behind him and all around his feet the court rolls lay in an untidy mess. Later, after the proceedings, he would collect them all up and push them into long pipes where they would remain in safe keeping in the Lord's chamber.

The children watched the clerk scribble whilst a tall, grey-haired man entered the room. He looked haughty and arrogant and he wore dark robes the colour of a stormy night. In his left hand he held a great staff of elm, the sign of his office within the household. His name was Thomas Galliard, the hated Steward of the Manor. He raised his bony hand to the air, stamped his staff upon the flagstones and asked for silence.

The chatter swiftly subsided and his Lordship, Richard de Calne entered the hall. He was a tall, noble looking man and though flecks of grey shone out from his dark hair, no signs of age

were visible on his proud face. He wore a red velvet tunic and a fur-lined surcoat with wide sleeves. Around his throat, a beautiful silver clasp held a rich woollen cloak in place. He calmly sat down upon a high-backed, elaborately carved, wooden chair, glanced briefly toward the children and then looked down upon his vassals.

For the next long hour the children sat in silence as Sir Richard dealt with a series of crimes and disputes. They watched in wonder as he received gifts of heriots, such as cows and pigs, from eager sons keen to inherit their father's land, but their boredom grew as he listened to complaints about the church tithes and taxes. Finally, he dealt with the punishments that were due and once again the children's interest grew.

The first man brought forward for such a sentence was so shabbily dressed his ragged tunic clung to him for dear life. He had grey stubble on his chin and a hollow face and his dark, deep-set sunken eyes blinked constantly under the bright light of the glowing torches that lit the court.

"Walter of Tostock, My Liege," Galliard addressed Sir Richard. "He was caught poaching deer from Norton Wood," the steward sneered with contempt as he read out the accusation.

"Is this true Walter?" Sir Richard's voice was firm.

The man slowly raised his eyes to meet his

gaze. "Aye Sire."

"Why did you do it?" His Lordship enquired.

"Hunger Sire, pure hunger," the villein replied. "I was might hungry and my wife and children were near starving."

"Galliard," spoke Sir Richard, "make sure this man is put to work at the mill for the rest of the year."

"But my Lord," the steward intervened, "he has committed a grievous crime against you. He must be properly punished."

"You think working alongside the dreadful smell of Barnet the Miller is not punishment enough?" Sir Richard retorted.

The Hundred Court erupted into laughter. All, that is, except for the miller himself, who stood at the back of the crowd, looking indignant. Walter smiled. He knew that anyone working at the mill always got more than their fair share of bread and he and his family would not go hungry again. Sir Richard knew that Walter wouldn't need to steal his deer either. But Thomas Galliard was fuming! He glared at Walter and then at Sir Richard but knew better than to contradict his Lordship, especially in public, so he held his tongue and called up the next case.

"My Lord, I present William Tallow and Heff Greenleaf." Two villagers walked forward arguing noisily with each other. "They are disputing the ownership of a particularly fine horse," Galliard stated irritably.

"There's no dispute, she's mine I tell you!" shouted Heff Greenleaf. He was a large, beast of a man and he towered threateningly over the smaller Tallow, who turned to face him. "No she ain't Greenleaf! She's mine."

"Quiet!" Sir Richard's voice echoed through the hall and the two men stopped their bickering immediately. "I have an idea," Sir Richard rose from his chair and took his sword from his scabbard. "There appears to be only one way to settle this dispute." His blade gleamed under the light of the torches and he ran his fingers along its sharp edge. "We should cut the beast in two and you can have half each."

"No!" cried Tallow. "Let him have it but don't destroy her, she is too beautiful for that." Heff Greenleaf smiled, he would not have cared if Sir Richard had killed the horse, he was just determined not to see Tallow end up with her. But Greenleaf was in for a shock.

"Well," said Sir Richard, "it's all clear to me now." He looked down upon the two men and then spoke to William Tallow. "This horse is yours, for you would rather have lost it than see it killed and that confirms you are its rightful owner." Tallow smiled and thanked Sir Richard.

"As for you Greenleaf," his Lordship turned his attention to the larger man, "a day in the stocks will be your reward and make sure you do not come before me again for a good long while; I don't forget such callous behaviour."

The two men were hurriedly dismissed by the steward, who then turned and spoke to his master. "I see you have King Solomon's touch this morning Sire," Galliard smirked as he whispered the reference to the wise, biblical ruler.

"It would appear so Galliard," Sir Richard replied abruptly.

Two guards in the blue tunic of the de Calne household then gripped the arms of a prisoner and marched him slowly forward. The captive was a tall, bearded man and he walked slowly through the hall in pain, his hands tightly bound behind him.

"Is this Thatcher?" Sir Richard asked.

"Yes Sire," said the steward. "He is accused of murder My Liege".

"I know what he is charged with Galliard," and he turned his gaze upon the accused man. "Well Thomas Thatcher, we have a number of witnesses who claim you stabbed Samuel Sycamore to death after a dispute over a dice game. How do you plead?"

The bearded man looked tired and drawn, he had already spent a number of nights in the prison at Wyken manor.

"It is the truth My Lord. I slew him with my thatching knife. My anger got the better of me."

Sir Richard's face now sunk also. "Then I have no choice," he stated sadly. "You will be hanged in the morning." The two liveried guards took the man away, his head bent low in sorrow as Sir Richard turned to his steward and murmured his thoughts. "Such a waste of life," he sighed.

"You have no option Sire. It is the law - an eye for an eye sayeth the Lord."

"Yes I know Galliard, I just wish there was a better way."

As Sir Richard signed the death warrant, Thomas Galliard cast his beady eye upon the green children and called them forth. "My Lord, I present the Green Children of Woolpit."

"Thank you, Galliard." His Lordship had been waiting for this moment. He turned back to his steward, "Now you can all leave us."

"My Lord, are you sure? They may be dangerous!" exalted Galliard.

"Do they look dangerous?" Sir Richard was growing angry. "They look terrified to me."

"My Lord, it may be just that fear that provokes an attack. A captured beast is very unpredictable!"

"They are not captured and they are not beasts Galliard!"

"But Sire, even Master Simeon . . . "

"Enough!" bellowed de Calne as he shot a glance towards his son. "Simeon is young and has much to learn. Now leave us!"

With a great amount of fuss and complaint the large crowd bustled out of the hall and went back to their homes disappointed. Many of them had only come to the Hundred Court to hear the strange children speak and now they were all being sent home.

As the hall emptied Sir Richard rose from his chair and turned to his strange visitors.

"Come forward children," he smiled down at them. "I thought we could talk better in peace and quiet and I am sure you do not wish to be looked upon by such a crowd."

"Thank you," the children answered in unison.

"Now tell me," Sir Richard continued, "who found you?"

"Cob . . . Cob Fletcher," the words trembled from the girl's lips.

"Well, Fletcher is a good man and it was fortunate that you fell into his hands. Yet now you are in mine!" The words sounded ominous, Sir Richard embodied a feeling of power and yet his eyes belied warmth and kindness.

But for all his authority and for all his delicate questioning, like Cob Fletcher before him, Sir Richard could find out little about the children and eventually gave up his probing. "Well," he said, "for the present I hope you will take comfort here at Wyken. I promise you will be well fed and well looked after." The two children smiled, though they both thought they would be happier back at the Fletcher's cottage.

"We are very fortunate," he continued, "for here, within the very walls of this Manor House, we have someone who has great learning and experience and if he cannot help you, then I fear no-one can." He looked down thoughtfully upon his young charges. "Would you like to meet him?"

The children nodded. "Good," Sir Richard took their hands in his and led them from the Hall. "Then I will take you to him."

9: The Magpie

~ The owl is wise, but the magpie is cunning ~

The children followed Sir Richard down a narrow passageway and then up a long, winding, spiral staircase. When they reached the top they turned left and went along another narrow corridor. Then, his Lordship stopped abruptly in front of a door and with a grin turned to face them. "Now I will introduce you to a very special friend of mine. I call him 'la Pie,' which is French for magpie."

The door opened very slowly, and as the children peered inside a throng of candles threw out a fiery light into the dim corridor. As they stared into the chamber they quickly realised why the occupant had gathered his strange nickname for the room was littered with a host of trinkets just like a magpie's nest. There were scrolls, books, manuscripts and maps lying on tables, tottering on bookshelves and piled up in towers upon the floor. There were dried flowers, branches from trees and bunches of herbs hanging from the ceiling. Wooden chests were spilling out statues, weapons, banners and pennants. Religious relics, glass bottles full of strange powders and liquids all sat precariously on a narrow shelf in the far corner of the room. And all around the chamber,

69

bright tapestries were hung, displaying a wealth of colour and action. Wonderful cubic patterns from the Holy Land, the death of King Harold at the Battle of Hastings, the slaying of Grendel and the glory of King Arthur all loomed out from the torch lit walls.

Somewhere, behind all this clutter, a figure moved and then, in front of the dancing flames in the small hearth at the far end of the chamber, an aged figure turned to greet them with a smile. Deep lines were furrowed on his temple and a wispy white beard grew upon his chin, but his eyes were blue and lively.

"This is Nathaniel Drinkstone," Lord Richard stated. "Keeper of the Chronicles of Wyken Manor, master of local lore and a good friend. And, as you can see, a man keen to spend all the wealth of Wyken, on providing light for himself!"

The old man chuckled, rose to his feet and limped toward them with his arms open to welcome the visitors in. "All these candles are not an extravagance Richard, my eyes are not what they were and I am already working on the case of our young friends here." He moved a pile of books from a long narrow bench and ushered the children to sit down. Sir Richard stood next to him as he took his turn to question them. "Now," the old man's voice was warm and gentle, "tell me all about yourselves."

But instead of speaking, the green girl jumped up onto the bench and searched carefully through the bunch of herbs that hung from the ceiling. She quickly found what she wanted and pulled out three or four strands from a long straggly plant. Then she crossed to the hearth and threw them in the fire.

Within seconds the small chamber was full of a clear, green mist and then one of the tapestries on the wall seemed to come to life. Sir Richard and Nathaniel watched in wonder as the mail-clad warriors from the Battle of Hastings vanished and through the green haze a new scene appeared. Now they saw a great forest and through the trees they perceived stick figures moving. The people were running from some unseen danger. Then they watched as a sparkling crown of leaves fell to the floor and then there came the darkness. Moments later, the mist cleared and when they looked again the tapestry was as it had been and they saw once again the Saxon King with the arrow embedded in his eye.

"As I have told his Lordship here and as I told the villagers of Woolpit, that is all I remember." The green girl spoke softly and sadly and Nathaniel felt the sorrow deep within her and whilst the children turned away to stare in wonder at a strange bubbling experiment on the

71

table, Sir Richard turned to meet Nathaniel's eye.

"Did you see what I saw Nat?" His Lordship asked the old man. "Figures and trees and crowns, alive within the tapestry!"

"Yes, I believe so!" he answered.

"What was it Nathaniel?" His Lordship looked pale with astonishment.

"I do not rightly know," the old man looked bemused, "perhaps she is explaining what happened to them."

"How is it that they have never encountered men like us before, Nat?"

"I am not entirely sure My Lord, but I do know that the Conqueror's Domesday Book stated that one half of all England was covered with forest. It was said that a squirrel could cross from the Severn to the Wash without putting his feet on the ground," he replied deep in thought.

"Yet much has been cut down for crops and settlement since then?" asked Sir Richard.

"Here in the south perhaps, but in the north and the west there still lie great trackless forests. Who knows what lies in the heart of those dark domains, Sire."

"I guess you're right Nat. From what I can tell from their speech it seems as if a whole settlement, even a Kingdom, lies hidden in the woodlands; untouched, separate to our world."

The old man thought hard upon the subject and scratched his forehead. "There's clearly something wrong. They speak as if their father is lost or in great danger. They must find him and quickly it would seem."

"I want to help Nat, I have already sent out riders to try and gain some news, but I do not really know what to do with them!" Sir Richard replied, looking pleadingly at his aged friend.

The old man turned back to the children and looked down upon his odd visitors. "Let's start at the beginning then shall we. You know my name but I do not know yours."

"I am Clyssa," the girl replied.

"And I am Hylasses," said the boy. "That at least I do remember," he added.

"And what do your names signify?" Nathaniel asked inquisitively.

"I do not understand what you mean," the girl answered.

"Well, I was born in the next village which is called Drinkstone - hence my surname. Lord Richard's family is named after the town of Calne in Normandy." Sir Richard elegantly bowed before them and they laughed.

"Other names come from the jobs people do," Nathaniel continued ignoring his Lordship's comical display. "A Fletcher produces arrows. Your friends the Fletchers were the finest arrow makers in the county once. Cob still makes a good flight for hunting."

"I know," the green girl smiled. "I was nearly on the end of one!"

"Well, the Coopers, Smiths, Weavers and Tilers are all named after the trades they do."

"I see," the girl replied. "Well then, I suppose our names refer to living things - plants and trees as you call them."

"So, if you could point out the plants that you are named after, then we could find out what they are called in our language?"

"I suppose so," the girl answered.

Nathaniel jumped off his stool in excitement and moved quickly across the stone floor to a dusty pile of manuscripts. He reached down and carefully collected a great hidebound book and returned to his desk. "This book is a record of the natural world. A dear old friend of mine, William of Rougham, compiled it. He was a Benedictine Monk at the great Abbey of Walsingham and it was his lifelong study; he left it to me when he died." Nathaniel's eyes twinkled as he reflected upon his lost friend but he stirred himself from his thoughts and opened the great volume. "Now then children, let's see if we can christen you shall we?"

The two children peered over the old man's shoulder as he carefully turned the pages.

"There!" the green boy shouted excitedly. "That is the tree I am named after."

"I see," said Nathaniel, and he continued turning the pages.

"And over there, up in the far corner of that page," the girl spoke excitedly, "that drawing is the same as the plant I am named after." She smiled at the old man and he in turn grinned at Sir Richard.

"Well, at least now we know what to call them!"

10: Simeon

~ A jealous farmer harvests only sorrow ~

"Hickory!" A cruel laugh echoed through the upper hall of Wyken Manor as Simeon de Calne made clear his amusement. It had been the hickory tree that the boy had pointed to in Nathaniel's book just as his sister had indicated the fern plant.

"Hickory!" Simeon repeated harshly, "We call that the pignut. That's a good name for you!" The green boy turned to face Simeon as the two boys passed each other at the top of the staircase. The boy looked angry. He did not like the way Simeon shouted at him, but as he moved forward towards him, Simeon thrust out his arm and pushed him hard in the chest. For a brief moment, Hickory balanced on the top step but then he lost his footing, slipped and fell headlong down the spiralling stairs.

He tumbled and thudded down the hard wooden steps until he finally crashed to the bottom. Dazed and groggy, he raised his head upward and a thin trickle of blood ran from a cut above his eyebrow. On hearing the disturbance, a servant ran out to see what had happened. As he helped Hickory to his feet, Sir Richard and Fern appeared at the doorway just in time to see

Simeon retreating from the staircase and heading outside.

As they sat Hickory on a stool, the girl wiped the blood from his forehead but Sir Richard paced the hallway in thought and then bellowed, "I will deal with my son!"

"No, leave him," the girl replied, in answer to Sir Richard's anger. "He fears us, I think."

"Even so," his Lordship marched to the doorway, "he must be punished!"

❧❧❧

Outside, a soft, summer rain splattered quietly on the cobbles of the courtyard where Simeon made ready his falcon, Icarus for an afternoon's hunting. He tied the bird's claws down upon his wrist and placed a leather hood over its eyes. The bird settled instantly listening intently to the sounds around it as its sight was extinguished.

Inside the Manor House, Sir Richard gazed out of his chamber window upon his wayward son and felt only anger and confusion. He'd tried desperately to love him but Simeon's birth had been the reason for his mother's death and Sir Richard had loved Alice de Calne more than mere words could express. The boy's eyes may have matched his mother's, his fair hair may have mirrored hers, but when Sir Richard looked Simeon in the face, he saw only his wife's pain and suffering and it hardened his heart. When the boy had fallen under the callous sway of Thomas Galliard, Sir Richard had let him go, but now he realised, there was still time to save his son from taking the wrong paths in life.

"Simeon!" Sir Richard bellowed from the window next to the courtyard. "Come to my chamber immediately!"

Reluctantly, the boy put his falcon back on its perch and made his way inside. What did his father want now? He didn't understand why he picked on him; he worked hard with the broadsword and rode well at the quintain. He had learned his letters, he knew how to behave at the table and he hunted with skill and prowess. Yet somehow it was never enough to please him!

"What you did was inexcusable!" Simeon stood silently before his father, his face downcast, staring defiantly at the stone floor. "You might have killed the boy," Sir Richard roared at his son. "You are forbidden to hunt for a month."

Simeon looked up sharply, "But Father," he pleaded, "the season has just begun and my new falcon has only just been trained. It will lose everything it has learnt if it lies idle for a month."

"So be it Simeon. You will just have to re-train it." Sir Richard's anger was only too evident. "Think about that young man. Perhaps you can be re-trained as well. Remember a Knight and a Lord need to show compassion, patience and wisdom as well as force and strength. Now leave me!"

Simeon cast his eyes back to the stone floor and gloomily left his father's chamber. As he closed the door behind him he heard the green children's voices away along the corridor and under his breath he muttered an oath of revenge.

11: Honeycakes

~ Never argue in the presence of bees ~

The children spent a restful night sleeping in a chamber, high up in the top floor of the Manor house. Sir Richard had hoped it would be like sleeping up in a tree and Nathaniel had filled their room with plants and had spread reeds over the floor to make them feel as comfortable as possible.

The following morning, Sir Richard found the children struggling with their breakfast. He stared down thoughtfully as they sat around the hall table looking miserable. "Aren't you hungry?" he said as he looked at the unfinished food on their platters.

"We don't eat this," Hickory exclaimed as he pushed away his ham.

"We're used to nuts, berries and mushrooms," Fern added. "I'm sorry but we do not eat animals."

"I see," replied Sir Richard. "Well, I am sure we can tempt you to something new. Come with me and let me introduce you to someone very special. In fact most people here at Wyken believe her to be the most important member of the household, myself included." He took the children by the hand and led them outside through a narrow corridor and into a large room separated from the main house.

"This is the kitchen. It is well away from the house in case some fool of a cook burns us all down!" Sir Richard said this last sentence just loud enough for the large figure chopping onions in front of a great fire to hear.

"I'm the only person in this cold, miserable country that is worthy enough to cook on a fire your Lordship," the woman replied as she turned to meet the visitors to her domain.

She was altogether round in shape, including her wide, open face. She had a ruddy complexion with girlish rosy cheeks, though she was older, much older than Sir Richard.

"This is our cook, Mary of Chalois; she is from the far away land of Gascony and she cooks food fit for a king."

"Of which you are not Sir Richard, so one wonders why I remain in this dark, damp England of yours."

"It must be for love of your Lord," Sir Richard replied with a cheeky smile.

"It certainly is not for the weather!" Mary of Chalois answered and beamed a mock smile at Sir Richard as she wiped onion tears from her eyes.

Suddenly, a cold morning breeze burst in, as the door that led from the kitchen down to the apiary, was thrown wide open.

"Damned bees!" the slight figure of Simeon de Calne rushed into the room holding his left hand tightly. He pushed roughly passed the two green children.

"Careful boy!" Sir Richard shouted. "You'll have them in the broth!"

"I've been stung Father."

"And I can guess how. Youv'e had your hand in the hives again, haven't you? Grasping greedily for fresh honeycomb. When will you ever learn Simeon?" Sir Richard sounded exasperated.

Instinctively, Fern ran to the kitchen table and picked up a chunk of sliced onion. She turned and gripped hard upon Simeon's wrist.

"Get off you beast!" he shouted but before he could stop her she pushed the onion onto the sting. Simeon cried out with the initial shock but then all pain left his hand, he felt nothing. It was as if the bee sting had never existed!

"It's stopped hurting Father!" He looked up in amazement at Sir Richard.

"Then say thank you to Fern," Sir Richard replied.

"No!" the boy exclaimed. "It's some evil, green magic. My arm will probably drop off later!" With a mixture of fear and hatred he backed away from the girl, pulled his hand free and ran back outside.

"Ungrateful little wretch!" muttered Mary as she slipped out of the kitchen and into the buttery. When she returned, she carried in her arms a great wooden tray. Upon this platter were a dozen or so honeycakes. She picked off two and put them in a wooden bowl. Collecting a pan from the stove, Mary poured a rich warm almond curd over the cakes. She sat the children down around the table and put the dish before them and handed them two wooden spoons. "Tuck in," she encouraged the children.

With an air of trepidation the children slowly approached the dish, but they wanted to please the cook, so they started to eat the honeycakes. Within seconds, the joy on their faces was all too evident and Hickory's grin was a pleasure to behold. The boy clearly had a sweet tooth!

"Not too many now or you will not eat your luncheon!" Mary tried to restrain the children as they looked over to the platter and the remaining pile of the pastries.

"I think we may have converted you," Sir Richard smiled and then he too joined in devouring the rest of the honeycakes.

12: Firefly

~ All life has words but not all men listen ~

After an unspoilt luncheon, Sir Richard took the green children out to the stables and as the sun stood high in the midday sky, they crossed the cobbled courtyard and turned towards the wooden outbuilding, which housed Wyken's horses. Behind them, staying close to the edge of the enclosure there was movement but Sir Richard and the children sensed nothing as the slight, sly figure stepped out of the shadows and followed them.

"Do you ride?" asked Sir Richard as he opened up one of the stable doors.

"Ride upon what?" the children answered.

His Lordship laughed, "Upon horses of course. Perhaps, it is about time you learnt," he said and he strode over to the stable and led out a beautiful black stallion. "This is Thatch," he proudly stated. "I've just bought him from the market at Bury St. Edmunds. He's stunning don't you think?"

The children nodded in agreement as they stared at the noble looking beast.

As they turned from the livery door, the shadowy shape crept out from the corner of the stable and stood unseen behind the horse.

Silently, it lifted a small leather whip and with all its might brought it down on Thatch's hindquarters. With a sudden cry of pain, the steed reared up on its two back legs and then bolted, right towards the children.

"Thatch!" screamed Sir Richard, but it was too late. The stallion was out of control and in utter confusion he bore down upon the two slight, green figures that stood before him. Fern and Hickory turned to meet the charging horse and it looked as if they would be trampled underfoot, crushed beneath the great stallion's iron hooves, but just before he was on top of them he pulled to a halt and sparks flew as his horseshoes scraped on the cobbled ground and the screech of metal on stone splintered through the courtyard.

It was Fern that had brought him to heel, her grey-eyed stare had mesmerised the stallion and once he had settled she gently took hold of his reins, stroked him and whispered into his ear. The horse appeared to neigh in reply and then she led him quietly over to Sir Richard.

"His name is actually Firefly," she said quietly as she handed Sir Richard the reins.

"How do you know that?" he asked in sheer amazement.

"Because he told me of course," Fern replied.

"Can you not speak to the animals then?" Hickory interrupted, in an amused tone.

"Why no!" Sir Richard answered. "No man can."

And with that both children laughed out loud and it sounded like a merry waterfall flowing down over rocks. Then, it seemed that Thatch, or Firefly, laughed along too and poor Sir Richard stood dumbfounded in his own courtyard.

After the laughter subsided he took the horse's reins and walked over to Fern.

"I am giving him to you," said Sir Richard.

"What do you mean?" asked Fern.

"He is yours. He belongs to you."

"He belongs to no-one!" she stated in surprise. "He's free to do as he will. If he lets me ride upon his back, that is fine, but I cannot command him, only ask him."

Sir Richard looked bemused. "In our world, animals are bought and sold like goods. They are owned by a master. Even people can be owned."

"It's not right!" It was the green girl's turn to be perplexed now.

"I think we have much to learn from you," Sir Richard cast his eyes to the sky, "but sadly I do not think many men will listen." As they turned to lead Firefly back to his stable the shadowy figure that had spooked the horse, silently slipped away unnoticed.

A faint evening sun lit the window seat in the solar where Sir Richard and Nathaniel sat playing out the last throes of a tense game of chequers. Ancient faces from the rich, woollen tapestries above them watched in awe as his Lordship's instinctive cunning battled with Drinkstone's aged wisdom in what had proved to be a stimulating game.

"My riders have returned to tell of many strange and wild stories, Nat," his Lordship jumped over the old man's last counter and smiled in victory.

"There always are my Lord," Nathaniel answered as he rose from the game to poke the dying fire.

"It seems the King of France has made a pact with the devil!" Sir Richard slowly sipped his goblet of wine.

"Again!" said Nathanial. "That is his fourth treaty with him this year."

"And a great black bull has rampaged through the streets of London killing many townsfolk," Sir Richard continued.

"There has always been trouble with traffic in the city," Nathaniel answered wryly.

"The last despatch stated that a witch had been hung in Norwich along with her dog."

"That is not good news," Nathaniel looked perturbed. "Witch-hunts are violent and dangerous and many innocent victims get caught up in the fervour."

"I know," Sir Richard replied, "and I hope that kind of thing does not spread this way."

"But there is nothing to help our young guests?" Nathaniel asked.

"No, nothing Nat, and that concerns me greatly." Sir Richard looked to the hearth. "Soon others will begin to ask about the children for I cannot keep their existence hidden for long."

"Then we must pray that some news comes quickly." Nathaniel finished his own wine and put out the fire.

13: Scrab Apples

~ The fruit that is bruised, is not yet rotten ~

Two small heads, one chestnut-brown and curly, the other flaxen-haired and straight, bobbed over the wall that separated the courtyard from the stable block, watching the scene below them with great interest.

Down on the cobbles Simeon de Calne and his friends were busy practising their knightly skills. In one corner Hugo Pomfrey, a fat rosy-cheeked boy, defended stoutly with a shield as Simeon rained down blows upon him with his broadsword. By the stable wall the tall, spindly figure of young Caspar de Joinville lunged at the angular frame of Ralf Jackamon with a lance.

Sunlight shimmered on their chain mail, swords and shields flashed brightly and wolfish howls followed the crashing blows they made upon each other as the fighting got ever more violent. Hugo suffered a heavy smash to the shoulder and dropped his shield with a thud, Ralf slipped and banged his knee hard on the cobbles and then a cruel and callous laughter boomed out as both Simeon and Caspar finally knocked their weaker opponents to the ground.

From their hiding place, Till and Hickory watched with awe at the skills displayed by

Simeon and his nest of vipers. The older boys below them were tall and proud, sons of Norman nobles and they fought with a hard, direct strength that impressed Till Fletcher. Hickory too, was transfixed by the way they nimbly swung their weapons and how they lunged and parried like fighting stags.

While the practice went on, however, the boy's aggression rose and a vicious spitefulness entered into their warlike play. Hugo's nose was bloodied, Caspar's fingers were trodden on when he dropped his lance, even Simeon, the ablest of them all, had been knocked to the ground more than once. When the boys disrobed from their armour and began to brawl, Till and Hickory decided it was time to retreat.

"I'm hungry," Till whispered as they moved off the stable wall.

"Let's go then," replied Hickory, "I know where to get some food."

But suddenly, Till lost his balance. He fell clattering onto a mound of kitchen pans, which had been left out to dry in the sun. Below them, the four wrestling boys looked up to see a green face dodge out of view.

"Pignut!" Simeon hurled out the insult like a spear. Instantly, they broke free from their fighting and with their blood rising, they scrambled up the wall to chase the two younger boys. As Hickory dropped deftly to the floor on the other side he helped Till to his feet and shouted "Follow me!"

They headed for the far corner of the gardens of Wyken Manor where there was a small, well-tended orchard. In his short time at the Manor House, Hickory had found this place more homely than anywhere else. He was uncomfortable with the grandeur of the great hall, had found his chamber too enclosing and though he loved being in the kitchen, not least for the honeycakes, it was always busy and noisy. So, it was here under the spreading limbs of the apple trees, that he considered his 'secret' place.

It had always been a flourishing orchard, where some eighty or so apple trees had grown for many generations. There was the green 'Newtown Pippin', the golden 'Tolman', the large fruits of 'Golden Russet', and the small but sweet 'Summer Paradise'. They all yielded a good crop every October and each autumn the inhabitants of Wyken Manor looked forward to feasting on apple pies and drinking their share of cider. But Sir Richard and many others had noticed that this year in particular the apples looked wonderful and all of Wyken would drown in a flood of sweet cider this yuletide.

As the two boys scarpered down the gravel path to the orchard and made their way, quietly, into the middle of the trees, they looked behind to make sure that they had lost Simeon and his gang. Then, Hickory reached up into the branches, picked off two bright green apples and sat down next to Till with their backs against a tree trunk. The apples were not quite ripe but they bit into them hungrily and savoured the fresh, sour, green taste in their mouths; it reminded Hickory of the greenwood and he closed his eyes and tried to think of home.

"I'm used to eating scrawny, little scrab apples," Till mused as he finished his Golden Russet with delight. "I don't think I've ever had one as large as that before."

"All apples are born from your scrab apple," Hickory spoke knowingly. "You should bury them in the ground and leave them until the dead season has gone, then they will be red and sweet."

"What is the dead season?" Till enquired.

"When the trees lose their leaves, when the forest turns grey and everything dies."

"Oh, you mean Winter," Till replied. "I hate it . . . nothing decent to eat!"

The boys continued to chat idly and the morning began to slip away, but at the far end of the orchard a number of pairs of eyes watched the two boys closely. Simeon's nest of vipers had found them!

"Pignut!" the stinging nickname bellowed out again, it snapped Hickory and Till out of their chatter, just in time for them to see the boys charging towards their hiding place. They saw that they all carried long willow sticks in their hands and the boys knew if they were caught they were in for a beating. Hickory and Till sprang to their feet and darted away!

They dodged in and out of the trees of the orchard with lightning speed but their pursuers, under the leadership of Simeon, had fanned out like a hunting pack and they were closing in on them. Till then made the mistake of looking back to see where their hunters were, he caught his foot on a stump and crashed to the ground. Simeon and his vipers instantly smelt blood and gave out a great whoop as they came in for the finish. Seeing what had happened, Hickory grabbed hold of the nearest tree trunk and in his own strange language gently whispered to it.

All of a sudden, the apples, that were not nearly ready to drop, started plummeting to the ground at great speed. It was as if the trees were throwing their fruit at the boys. They thumped onto heads, crashed down upon shoulders and backs and thudded against the upheld hands that the boys threw up in a vain attempt at defence.

The gang cried out in pain. Hugo slipped and fell, Caspar became so confused he ran into a trunk, Ralph Jackamon swore and shouted at the trees whilst Simeon just ran. Eventually, they all managed to escape from the orchard but by the time they had cleared the final trees they had been well and truly splattered in peel and pips. Bruised, battered and defeated they slunk away and in the background all they could hear was Till and Hickory's merry laughter.

14 : Revelations

~ *Names can be dangerous things* ~

The great tower of St. Mary's Church of Woolpit was a beautiful sight and it rose radiantly above the village and the fields around, like a beacon of hope rising high to touch the very face of God. On this bright morning, as the bells rang out calling the people to prayer, two new visitors were brought into its welcoming arms.

Although Sir Richard was not a very religious man, like all good Christians, he attended church every Sunday and on this particular morning he had decided to take Fern and Hickory along to St. Mary's to see if they recognised any of the rituals or beliefs that they would find there. He knew sitting through one of Brother Cuthbert's long latin services was a hard enough task for any children, let alone ones that were green and lived in the forest, but he was curious to see their reaction.

At first, the children were far more interested in seeing Till and Meg, who had also been dragged along that morning. But as they quietly walked under the porch and into the nave they slowly began to notice their surroundings.

All around them colourful paintings dazzled

in the candlelight and carvings and sculptures peered down upon them from the high ceiling above. The children felt quite uneasy when they stared upon the scenes from the bible of hell and damnation and the odd shaped gargoyles that leered down upon them, but the Fletchers sat with them and re-assured them and they watched with interest as Sir Richard and Simeon knelt before the priest and took Holy Communion. They noted the solemn tone of the services before them and they understood the importance of the ceremonies to the people around them, but like many of the children within the church that morning they soon grew bored and restless and the only praying they did was for Brother Cuthbert to stop droning on.

It was as Sir Richard had expected. The children knew nothing of churches, priests and the importance of religion. On questioning them, it soon became apparent that they had no idea who Jesus was or what the bible told. Till Fletcher had explained a strange account of the Pope to them and they retold this as well as they could, but it was clear Christianity was not part of their home in the woods.

Simeon also noticed the children's lack of faith but he had other ideas about it. As he stood outside the church porch and watched them leave, holding hands with his father, he started to bring his ideas together. He thought about their understanding of herblore and the strange way they seemed to hold animals in their spell. He began to wonder about that morning's attack from the apple trees and he'd even heard his father talk of dancing figures in a tapestry. Simeon added all these strange events together and a plan at last began to formulate within his jealous mind.

"I have a name for you Master Simeon."

Thomas Galliard, appeared out of the darkness of the passageway and handed the boy a parchment scroll.

"Thank you Galliard," Simeon replied in a hushed voice. "I will not forget this."

"I hope not My Liege." And with that he slithered back into the shadows.

Simeon hurriedly unfolded the scroll, looked down eagerly upon the name written on it, and smiled. Softly, serpent-like he whispered the name to himself.

15: The Abbot

~ The crow is the cruellest of all the birds ~

"**W**hat pure rotten luck," thought Sir Richard, as the messenger from the Abbot of Bury St. Edmunds scurried away from Wyken Manor. "Trust him to be staying in his Summer Palace at Elmswell just when our green friends are here." With a feeling of doom, Sir Richard unrolled the scroll and read the command. It was short and direct: *'Bring the children to me'* and he knew he would have to concede to it straight away.

❧

As Sir Richard and the children entered the gates of the palace later that afternoon, a file of black hooded figures was just leaving the small chapel in the corner of the compound as the bells rang out to signify the end of Vespers. The children turned their faces away from the monks instinctively and gripped hard to de Calne's arms and the Benedictines, in their black habits, stared across the courtyard at the green visitors, like ghostly spectres emerging from the shadows.

Then, from the doors of the palace itself, a young novice, barely older than Fern, came to greet them. "I am brother Julian," the young monk said as he approached them.

"Whose brother are you?" asked Hickory innocently.

The novice looked bemused and then the children looked in wonder at the boy's head, and giggled at the bald patch upon his crown.

"Why do you laugh at me?" he asked crossly.

"You seem too young to be losing your hair," Fern replied.

"Oh, that is my tonsure," the novice monk answered as if that would answer their questioning.

"Your what?" cried Hickory.

"A tonsure is when a monk has the top of his head shaved so as to signify the crown of thorns worn by Jesus," the novice retorted indignantly.

The children both turned to Sir Richard quizzically. "Who is Jesus again?" said Hickory. At this, the novice looked visibly shocked. In fact the strange colour of the children had not concerned him half as much as this lack of basic Christian knowledge and his eyes indicated a sudden repulsion.

"He is our Lord and Saviour, the son of God," Sir Richard calmly replied and he turned upon the novice. "Now quickly lad, take us to the Abbot." The boy hurriedly led them past the herb gardens and the Abbot's maze, across a gravel courtyard and into the west door of the palace.

❧

Sir Richard was not looking forward to meeting up again with Abbot Guy, who was as harsh and as rugged as the west coast of Brittany, from whence he came. And his Lordship was not alone in his hatred of the Abbot either. There were few people in the diocese that had a good word to say about him, and sadly fewer still, who would stand up to his iron will.

The novice knocked timidly on the door of the inner sanctum of the palace and entered with trepidation as he led Sir Richard and the two children into a high-ceilinged chamber. In front of them on a large dais the Abbot's dark figure sat upon a beautifully carved seat. As they approached, two hooded attendants swooped down to the Abbot's side like bats and he slowly turned like a great crow to listen to their whispers.

Sir Richard instantly recognised some of the hushed Breton language that slipped from their lips and echoed faintly around the hall; words such as 'bugale gwer' meaning green children and 'vars' which meant wicked.

Then, the Abbot turned to them and his bitter Breton accent beat down upon them like a whip.

"So these are the green children of Woolpit, Sir Richard."

"Yes, your Worship," Sir Richard replied.

"Have you taken them to Mass?"

"Last Sunday."

"And how did they respond to that?" the Abbot asked coldly.

"They were as bored as all the other children there," Sir Richard's jovial tone annoyed the Abbot.

"So, they are Godless heathens then!" His voice echoed sternly through the chamber as he rose from his high backed chair, his robes fluttering like black wings. He stared coldly at the children and then crossed the stone floor to inspect them.

He looked them up and down like a hungry wolf in a henhouse. He took in their pale green skin, their deep and earthly grey eyes, their straight flaxen hair and their strange dress. His breath was stale and the children recoiled as he came close to them. "I find them very disturbing," he stated coldly. "They make me feel uncomfortable as if something 'val', or 'evil' as the English say, has entered this very room."

"I don't feel that at all," Sir Richard, replied defensively, his anger rising. He accepted the blindness and hypocrisy of the Church only because it seemed to keep peace in a troubled world but he felt instinctively protective to his young charges. God moves in very mysterious ways if this is one of his servants, he silently thought. "They are God's creatures as are you and I your Worship," he continued.

"No, de Calne, I believe they are servants of 'Diaul', the devil."

"Then you are a fool, your Worship. They are lost and lonely and until I can help them return to their homeland, they will stay with me!"

"On your head be it then, de Calne," the Abbot spat the words out. "But I warn you, no good will come of sheltering these creatures in Wyken Manor."

"Better that, than leave them to your care, where they'll no doubt be paraded as evil beasts to gain you even further unworthy renown," de Calne put a fatherly arm around the children and turned for the door. Fern and Hickory glanced back at the black figure as they passed out through the dark chamber and shuddered as the Abbot smiled at them.

⁂

Whilst they walked quickly out of the grounds of the Abbot's palace the children stared at a huge network of raised banks and mounds. Around these lay an elaborate square of willow fences and in the corners of the square there were tall wooden watchtowers.

Suddenly, from behind one of the banks a startled pair of eyes and a flash of grey fur disappeared underground. It was a rabbit!

"Why are those poor creatures kept in captivity?" Fern questioned Sir Richard.

"It is to encourage them to breed," he replied, "and of course to ensure that they do not escape into the wild."

"But why would the God-man want them?" Hickory responded, referring to the Abbot.

"He had this warren created to supply his household with meat and fur."

"You mean he eats them!" Fern looked shocked.

"I mean just that," Sir Richard suddenly felt a pang of guilt; he too liked nothing better than a good rabbit pie.

"It's so cruel!" Fern stated fervently.

Just then a small, hunchbacked figure clambered clumsily down from the nearest watchtower.

"Who is he?" whispered Hickory.

"I don't know his real name," muttered Sir Richard, "but he is known as Crookback and he is the warrener."

"What does he do?" inquired Fern.

"It's quite simple, his job is to keep the rabbits in and the poachers out. You see that quiver of arrows slung over his shoulder?" The children stared at the warrener. "Well, he may look clumsy but he has a crossbow up in that tower and he is one of the finest shots in this county. That's why there are so few poachers on these grounds."

The warrener had not taken his eyes off the children since he had spotted them and even as he continued to straighten a loose fence post his vigil did not end. The children suddenly remembered how Tam had gotten his one eye and they quickly held tight to Sir Richard's arms as they left the Abbot's domain.

16: Crookback

~When the stars are out, the fairies are about ~

For a few, brief midnight seconds nothing moved. No sounds could be heard and nothing could be seen. Then, two dark, almost invisible figures broke from their hiding place behind a hedgerow and ran unnoticed right up to the strange network of fences that lay directly ahead of them.

As they skipped over the outer willow hedges and zig-zagged through the complex rabbit warrens, a startled owl hooted out loud. Out of the darkness, heavy footsteps could be heard and a deep, gruff voice startled them. "I know you're out there," Crookback hollered, "I can smell you." And as his words fluttered on the wind a crossbow bolt whistled past Fern's left ear and embedded itself in the soft, dewy grass directly behind her.

But it was a stray shot, for all the warrener's fine words he couldn't see the children and they moved far too quickly for him. Even so, Hickory's hand trembled as he hurriedly took the knife that he'd borrowed from the Manor House kitchens, and started to undo the bindings of the fence. Within seconds, he had pulled down the willow barrier and a rustling of small paws indicated that the rabbits were running free towards them.

Crookback was seething as he listened helplessly to his rabbits escaping. Realising he had lost his animals only made him more determined to capture those responsible for the crime. At least then he could hand them over to the Abbot in the hope that it might make up for the loss of the rabbits. So, the warrener now put to work a tried and tested plan. He aimed to guide his poachers into the Abbot's maze, he knew the layout of the labyrinth like the back of his hand, and it was here that he caught his prey like a spider with its web.

Unknowingly then, Fern and Hickory found themselves being chased directly for the opening of the great maze. As they entered it they heard the warrener cranking the handle that wound the cord back on his crossbow.

"Quickly," Fern shouted, "this way." She darted off to the left and Hickory followed behind her. But he was too slow and Crookback, alerted by the noise, let fly an arrow as Hickory turned the first corner of the maze.

Whoosh! The shaft sped through the air like steel lightning. The iron tip of the crossbow bolt grazed across Hickory's thigh and he cried out in pain.

"Now I have you!" Crookback whooped

with glee, bent his hunched frame to use his body as a lever to rewind the weapon and made ready to fire another bolt.

"Are you alright?" Fern ran back to her brother and helped him to his feet.

"It is not deep," Hickory answered, "but it will slow me down."

A steady trickle of blood dripped from the wound and fell upon the ground.

"We must move on, I can hear him approaching and the moon's coming out. He's going to see us!" Fern looked back to the first turning of the maze. "The deeper we get into this maze the harder it will be to escape him."

"And I bet he knows every turn in the place, it wasn't by chance that he chased us this way. He did it deliberately. We're trapped!" Hickory sat back upon the floor in defeat.

"Not yet we're not," Fern exclaimed, "I have an idea."

Back at the entrance of the maze, the moon at last broke free from the shackles of the cloud cover. Now it will be easy, the warrener thought, as he came upon the spots of blood on the grass in the pale light. I can track the path of blood and it will lead me right to them. It doesn't matter if the Abbot gets his poachers dead or alive, as long as he gets them!

But the warrener was too confident, for Fern

was already putting her plan into motion. She touched the twisted limbs of the yew hedge and spoke softly to it as if it was another human being. Then she laid her body back against the wall of the maze and started to become as one with the hedge. Her hair seemed to transform into leaves, her arms and legs became branches and her fingers twisted into thorns. On seeing his sister metamorphosise, Hickory followed suit. Within moments, he too had melted into the background of the hedge and had become hidden deep within the green foliage.

They were just in time, for seconds later, breathing hard, the warrener came to the end of the trail of blood. He unsheathed his knife and made ready to capture his poachers . . . but they were not there!

"Impossible!" the warrener screamed. "They cannot disappear and yet the trail stops here." He scratched his head as he gazed at the wall of the maze in thought. "They did not tunnel underneath and they cannot fly. It's too thick and prickly to climb through so where in God's name have they gone?"

In his rage Crookback slashed at the maze with his knife narrowly missing Hickory's face. The yew hedge screamed with a pain that ran through the children. Fern wanted to break free from her hiding place and stop the hedge's suffering but Hickory gripped hard upon her wrist and wouldn't let her give herself up. They held their breath as the warrener ran up and down the path in frustration, but then as the moon slipped behind a cluster of clouds, all around them the maze began to move and a path opened up. Within seconds a clear trail lay before them and they broke free of the hedge and ran straight out of the maze and out of Crookback's trap.

The rustling movement of the shifting maze alerted Crookback. And as the moon came back out of hiding and shone down upon him once more, he turned back to the entrance of the maze to check his poachers had not escaped past him. But as he turned he found a wall of yew in his way. He blinked his eyes to make sure he was not seeing things. But no, a solid wall of hedge blocked his path.

He carried on forward at a trot, for he knew this maze and could take another path out easily enough. He turned right then left . "No!" he shouted in confusion. "That's not right!" For another wall now blocked him off.

"I don't understand!" he cried. Now he turned and ran. Sweat poured from his forehead and he began to grow dizzy as every path he knew turned into a dead end. Finally, he sat upon the ground, held his head in his hands and cried out for help. The spider was stuck in his own web!

The children grinned at each other as the warrener's desperate cries grew softer in the distance behind them. And then they were away across the fields back to Wyken as quietly and as swiftly as wild rabbits!

As the children passed back into the courtyard of Wyken Manor a single light burned away like the eye of the Cyclops. Far up in the east wing of the Manor House, Simeon de Calne sat hunched at the small lectern in his room. A candle flickered fitfully as he fumbled with the small pot of ink and hurriedly scratched his quill across the manuscript paper.

Then, he carefully dipped the nib into a bowl of lemon juice and wrote a message on the letter before him. He knew the lemon juice would make his words invisible and he also knew that the recipient of his letter only needed to hold the manuscript up to the light of a candle and the message would become readable again.

So now Simeon's revenge could at last be set in motion and this letter would be quickly despatched to the one man in Suffolk who could deal with his adversaries. For Simeon was writing to the notorious witchfinder . . . Silas of Wickham.

17: The Witch of Cotton

~ Pick holly to keep the witches away ~

"I'm innocent!" The old woman's voice screamed out the words in utter terror as her outstretched hand was pushed closer and closer to the scorching flames, but as she struggled, the two men holding her, fastened their grip. Then another shrill cry of agony shattered the solemn silence that wrapped itself around the tiny village of Cotton as her hand was thrust into the angry, red flames.

"The evidence is clear," a sinister voice echoed across the village green. "God has spoken to us." The dark figure held the old woman's blackened hand up for all to see. "The skin is burnt and blistered. This ordeal by fire shows that she is indeed a witch! Good people of Cotton, your suspicions were correct, you were right to call me."

Two gnarled, embittered, old women swapped grim smiles at their neighbour's misfortune as the witchfinder's voice of condemnation grew into a monstrous howling and the mob of villagers turned upon the old woman in a torrent of fury.

"Bring the priest!" the black-cloaked man called out, as he led the villagers to the hastily erected place of execution.

With her 'trial' over, the old woman wrapped a ragged cloth around her burnt hand to act as a makeshift bandage but before she had time to tie it she was dragged to the waiting gibbet. A noose was slipped roughly over her downturned head and in an instant her life was taken and her anguish ended.

An hour later, as the glowing embers of the fire died, a red sun mirrored its light as it slipped behind the swaying fields of barley. Two shadowy horsemen passed by the frail, hanging body without even a glance and slipped silently over the horizon. Coins jangled in their saddlebags as they took up the scent of their next prey. Finding witches was Silas of Wickham's business and he was finding it a very lucrative one indeed.

18: Nathaniel's Bond

~ Faces made of stone, smile forever ~

It was almost dark when a loud rapping broke the silence of Wyken Manor. A servant ran to the solar where Sir Richard was looking over the accounts of the demesne, tapped lightly on his door and entered.

"What is it?" Sir Richard asked anxiously.

"News my Lord, about the green children."

"Carry on."

"A rider has just returned from the coast. He awaits you in the hall."

Sir Richard quickly ran down the stairs and there in the torchlight a messenger shook rain from his cloak and brushed mud from his heavy leather boots. He looked up as his Lordship approached.

"My Lord," the messenger spoke with a strong Norman accent for he was one of Sir Richard's own household, "I have returned from the town of Woodbridge where I heard news of a wild green man that has been found off the coast near Orford."

"Did you see him?" Sir Richard questioned.

"No My Lord, he has been taken to the Royal Castle so that the Constable could speak to him."

"But he is green like the children?"

"So it has been reported, Sire."

"Excellent, Gaston. Now find your way to the kitchens for something to eat and drink and then get yourself to bed. And well done."

"Thank you, Sire." And with that the messenger left the hall.

Sir Richard looked up thoughtfully toward the chamber where the two green children slept. Surely this man must be connected to his strange young guests in some way. And perhaps he might even be their missing father!

Over the past week, Nathaniel Drinkstone had found himself becoming more and more attached to Fern and Hickory. He had never had children of his own and though he was nearer their grandfather's age than their father's, he felt a paternal pull towards them in their hour of need. So it was with a mixture of joy and sadness that he broke the news to them about the wild, green man.

Fern and Hickory bubbled with excitement at the discovery and they chattered away merrily in their own tongue all morning long. But it was not until they stood quietly in Nathaniel's chamber, with Sir Richard and the old man himself, that they actually began to realise the task that still lay ahead of them.

Nathaniel now reached down into the far corner of his room and tugged gently at a rolled manuscript that lay crushed under a small bronze chest. A sad, wizened bunch of dried herbs fell to the floor as the scroll came free. His aged hands unbound the ribbon that held it tight and he spread out the scroll across the oak table before the watching eyes. It was a map!

As his long, bony forefinger bore down upon the world that lay below, the veins on the back of Nathaniel's hand stuck out like contour lines. In the ensuing brief moments his finger passed over lands that would take days to cross.

Starting at a small, black cross his finger followed a thin blue line south cutting through circles indicating rising hills. As the finger pursued its course, the tiny scratchings of vegetation changed constantly. Grass to crops, through woods and marsh and scrub, until it all but disappeared into dense forest. The meandering blue line continued its journey south but now his finger left it behind and went due east. On it went past villages and over heathland until the track finally fell away and the finger came to an abrupt halt by the small crenellated symbol of a castle on the edge of nothingness - for after that there lay only the open sea.

The two children gazed upon the

outstretched map in sheer bewilderment for the mass of lines, names and symbols scattered over the parchment had meant nothing to them. In their world, maps were not needed as their own instinctive cunning was all they required, but here in this strange, treeless land they were forced to be guided by others.

"Well, there it is children!" Nathaniel's finger pointed downward. "Orford Castle - a royal stronghold and currently held in the stewardship of Bartholomew de Glanville."

"Not good news, I am afraid," Sir Richard interrupted. "I have met with him and he is a ruthless man - a danger to all those around him."

"How can we possibly hope to reach this place?" Fern asked. Hickory too, looked forlorn.

"What you need is a guide," Sir Richard said as he put an arm around his young wards. "Luckily I know just the man to lead you," and with a twinkling smile he turned to Nathaniel and the children's eyes looked up searchingly into the warm face of the old man.

"Yes, I will guide you," he said calmly. "We will leave tomorrow evening. I think it is a full moon."

"It is," the children replied in unison.

"It's a Hazel moon," continued Fern, "which means plenty of light; last month was a Holly moon and that would have been much darker."

"We'll travel by night then and avoid contact with other people," smiled Nathaniel. "I'm used to the colour of your skin now, but I'm not sure the rest of Suffolk will be, I also have some hooded cloaks that will help to hide your faces. They're made from strong, hardy Wyken wool so they'll also keep us warm at night, though I think I will benefit most from that. You two seem to have a natural strength that does not feel the cold!"

"Good, then everything is settled," Sir Richard stated.

"There is something that has been troubling me however," Nathaniel stroked the wispy white hairs of his beard. "What if your father is looking for you?"

"Yes, I suppose he may be searching for us," Hickory replied.

"What can we do to tell him where we are? We must pursue this path to the sea, it is our only hope," Fern sounded fretful.

"Do not despair lass, I have an idea," Nathaniel's face brightened. "We must leave a trail for your father to follow, it must be permanent and easy to find." He crossed the room, picked up his knapsack and plonked it on the table next to the map. Then he took out a chisel and a small hammer and passed them to the children. "Many years ago, before I was called away to the battlefield and the civil wars of King Stephen, I was apprentice to a stonemason."

"Yes, yes!" Sir Richard interrupted. "Ancient history!"

Nathaniel ignored his jibes and took back the tools. "We'll leave a path in the one building we are sure to find in every village we pass."

"What building is that?" asked Hickory.

"The church of course, every village has one and I can carve the face of a green man in amongst the carvings, statues and gargoyles. It will tell your father where we have gone if he ever picks up your trail."

"It's a good idea," Sir Richard looked pleased. "And if I find your father, I can set him off on the right path. He just needs to follow the trail of the green man."

"That's settled then," Nathaniel put his instruments back in his bag, "I'll start with St. Mary's tonight."

19: Endings and Beginnings

~ The track less worn, is the one to follow ~

"So, this is the end of our short friendship," Cob looked down upon the green children with a fatherly smile. It was dusk in the courtyard of Wyken Manor and the failing light only added to the sadness of their parting.

"No," replied Fern, "I think this is just the beginning."

"I hope so, for there are few people in this world who will ever touch our lives like you have."

A single tear fell from Fern's eye as she embraced him.

"I hope you find your father," he whispered gently in her ear. Then he turned to Hickory, "Well young man, you take care of your sister and perhaps some day we will meet again."

"I will teach my people how to play camp-ball," Hickory smiled and then he too embraced Cob.

As they made ready to leave, Martha handed the children parcels which contained some apples, a cheese and a fresh loaf and gave them both a kiss. Mary of Chalois waddled out from the kitchen and passed a neat bundle to Hickory. "Honeycakes!" she whispered to him and he grinned with glee as he thanked the old cook.

Sir Richard gripped hard upon Nathaniel's arm. "Take care my old friend, and be sure to return to us as soon as you see them safely despatched."

"I will, My Lord, and I will send news if I get the opportunity."

"Good luck children," said Sir Richard picking up Fern and Hickory in his arms. "I have had many visitors at Wyken but none like you. I will miss your merry laughter and your lively souls, though I am sure old Crookback will be pleased to hear of your departure," and his eyes twinkled knowingly.

Lastly, Till and Meg hugged the children and said their goodbyes. "I will not forget you," said Fern as she handed Meg a parchment scroll.

"Nor I you," Meg replied, "but what's this?"

"A few recipes for medicines," Fern answered, "Nathaniel wrote them down for me. I hope it helps you in times of need."

"Thank you," Meg replied and kissed her cheek.

Moments later, the three dark figures walked quietly down the track and out of the grounds of Wyken Manor. Just before they left the sight of those behind them, they turned and waved. Then, they left the muddied path, slipped across the newly ploughed top fields and were gone.

20: The Witchfinder

~ Evil rides under a full moon ~

Sir Richard was just finishing his evening meal when he looked down at his platter and gave a wry smile as he scooped up the last of the rabbit stew before him. He sat back comfortably in his chair and raised his goblet of wine in a silent toast.

Outside, a heavy rain drifted across the flat land and as the moon disappeared behind rain-laden clouds two dark horsemen entered the courtyard of the Manor. They got down from their mounts, drew back their hoods, strode across the cobbled stones and banged loudly upon the great oak door. A servant hurriedly let them in and a moment later Sir Richard's peace was broken.

"Who are you?" His Lordship did not like the look of the two strangers that stood before him.

"I'm Silas of Wickham, My Lord. Perhaps you have heard of me." The smaller man drew back his hood and shook his lank wet hair.

"Oh, I have," Sir Richard replied, "your reputation is well known."

"Good, then I want you to bring your green witches to me," Silas started to take off his sodden cloak.

"Don't get too comfortable, Wickham. There are no witches here. If you are referring to the green children that were found, then I am afraid you are too late, they have left!"

The witchfinder looked angry, "Where have they gone?"

"I have no idea!" Sir Richard's retort bit across the room.

"It's very unwise to meddle in the affairs of witches," Silas sneered.

"Your threats do not alarm me Wickham!"

"Then tell us the truth about these green devils."

"There's nothing to tell." Sir Richard held his anger at bay whilst he tried to convince the witchfinder of his story.

"The green children were here for a few days but last night they slipped back into the woods and returned to where they had come from."

"Where are these woods?" Silas pushed for more information.

"Far to the west as I understand, I don't suppose they will ever be seen again however, so you need not worry about them."

"I will be the judge of that de Calne."

"Well, I have told you all I know. I want you off my land now and if you take one step upon Wyken Manor again I'll set the dogs upon you!" Sir Richard's voice was hard and stern and the witchfinder knew when to back down.

"You have not heard the last of this de Calne," Silas spat out the words as he and his burly accomplice headed out of the chamber.

As the black figures stepped out into the spitting rain their horses were pulled up and Silas took the reins of his great steed 'Minotaur'. Just before he mounted the black horse a small shape left the doorway of the manor and called through the darkness to the witchfinder. After a brief conversation, Silas turned his horse not to the west but to the east and with his companion at the rear he rode off at speed. A shrill cackle tore through the night air like the cry of a hungry wolf and back in the doorway, Simeon de Calne allowed himself a smile of contentment.

21: Hue and Cry

~ *Freedom is a gift worth giving* ~

On a clear, black night, the stars came to life one by one, as if some great hand was lighting candles in the sky. A pale moon rose gently and reflected a shimmering light in the soft waters of the River Gipping. The silhouette of a heron stood tall and proud as it waded cautiously through the shallows searching for food. As something startled the bird it took to the sky in a singular effortless movement and it arched high into the night air and flew off further downstream to continue its wanderings undisturbed. Then, down by the river's edge three figures emerged out of the gloomy shadows and halted by the bank.

"Well, we have come about nine miles already," Nathaniel spoke in a hushed tone, "and we still have plenty of the night left to hide our journey."

The travellers had already skirted the sleeping villages of Harleston, Onehouse and Stow Thorney. Now they stood on the western bank of the river close to the small market town of Needham.

"I don't understand." Nathaniel stared down at the dark waters that lay before him.

"The river should not be as high as this. I had intended to cross here at the ford!" The old man's worried tone alarmed the children.

"Is there not one of your bridges nearby?" Fern asked.

"Yes," replied Nathaniel, "but it runs through the middle of the town and we cannot risk being spotted."

"Well, what can we do then?" Hickory's voice was drowsy with tiredness but as he finished his last words, a long, thin, dangling branch descended from above them and wrapped itself tightly around the boy's waist. Nathaniel thought they were being attacked but just as he reached out to Hickory's aid, Fern pulled him back.

"It's alright," she whispered to him. "It's just the willow. It's trying to help us."

Nathaniel looked again and before his eyes the willow tree seemed to have bent right over like an old man. By now it had actually raised Hickory up into the air by its slender branches and as they watched, the tree lifted the boy across the river and dropped him carefully on the other side. Hickory rolled over in the long grass on the far bank and then jumped up like a young deer to signal to them that he was okay. A split second later Fern found herself hoisted up and over the running waters and moments later she too was transported to the eastern bank.

Nathaniel stood quite still as the willow tree's branches now slipped around his waist. Its grip was firm and he felt secure but when the tree lifted him into the night air he yelled out in panic. In his fear he squirmed about like a fish on a line and then the willow lost its hold for a moment. Nathaniel closed his eyes as he hit the water headfirst but before he entered the flowing river fully, the willow caught hold of him again and flipped him onto the far bank with a bump. As the tree shook its branches dry and leant back into its normal posture, Nathaniel rolled over to find the children lying on their backs giggling away.

He shook his grey hair free of weed and algae and was about to reprimand them but as he opened his mouth to lecture them a water vole scuttled over him and the children burst out into a new fit of laughter. Nathaniel realised his dignity was lost, raised himself off the grassy floor, grabbed his knapsack and staff, and strode ahead. "Come on then," he muttered gruffly. "Let's get a move on."

The children followed him off into the darkness. But it was a good mile or two before their soft laughter could no longer be heard in the valley.

By the dawn's scarlet light the travellers had edged carefully round the tiny settlement of Coddenham and as the village came to life, they moved quickly to avoid being seen and came to rest in a thicket of elder trees, just to the east of the village. They laid their blankets upon the soft, dewy ground and in no time at all they fell into a deep and welcome sleep.

It was not long before the sun had arched high above and a breathless air hung limply in the sky. The warm morning turned into a hot and sultry afternoon but the travellers slept on and it was not until the whole day had passed that they finally awoke. By the time Fern and Hickory opened their eyes and drew themselves up, dusk had already begun to fall. They looked around and found that Nathaniel had a small fire going and over it, he was softly singing, whilst he cooked a stew of vegetables and wild garlic in his old iron skillet.

Far below them, in the freshly ploughed fields, voices suddenly broke through the old man's gentle song and bellowed out across the open valley. Nathaniel instinctively put out the fire and pushed the children to the floor, as the voices grew louder.

Still in a sleepy daze the children peered down from the edge of the woods to see a young man running desperately across the far end of the field. Behind him, still on the track, a flame-haired horseman and three other men on foot, were in hot pursuit.

"Why do they chase that man?" Fern whispered with a mixture of shock and horror etched upon her face.

"I suspect he is a runaway villein," Nathaniel answered.

"If he runs away from his manor and escapes to a town and avoids capture for a year and a day - he will be a free man."

"Are not all men free?" questioned Hickory.

"Certainly not! The Fletchers are villeins just like him," Nathaniel pointed to the running figure far below them.

"Then why do they not run away and become free?" Fern asked.

"That is because they are content. Sir Richard is a good master; perhaps this man is not so lucky. Perhaps his Lord is Alain the Red, Lord of Helmingham. He is said to be cruel and unjust. He must surely have a reason to run."

They looked down as the three running servants followed the horseman onto the field. He barked orders at them and slapped the whip down hard upon his steed and within moments was upon the runaway. The young man stumbled in the heavy clay of the ploughed field and then he fell headlong into the earth. As he tried to get to his feet the rider's whip lashed down wickedly upon his back and he cried out in agony.

Within minutes, the three servants had hold of him and when he finally rose from the earth a heavy chain was now tied around his ankles. His hands were bound and with his head downcast he was pulled to heel behind the horse. Solemnly, the master and his men left the field and made for the track below.

"What will happen to him Nat?" Hickory was shaken by the events.

"He will probably be beaten and fined and then he will be returned to his labours in the fields."

"I do not understand your world!" Hickory exclaimed.

"Sometimes children, neither do I," Nathaniel replied and he turned away to face the trees. "Let us then, enter your world. For a short time at least it would be good to escape the eyes of men." And with that the three of them slipped from the trees' edge and entered the very depths of the wild woods.

22: The Army of the Wild Wood
~ An east wind always blows cold and hard ~

It was well past midnight when the witchfinder turned to his accomplice. "You know why they're heading to Orford, don't you Girth?"

"I presume they want to take a boat to escape back to wherever it is they came from."

"Oh no Girth, they have other plans. They are looking for someone, that de Calne brat told me everything. He will make quite a callous brute when he grows into manhood."

"So why are they making for Orford?" Girth asked. "It's a godforsaken town and the Constable of the Castle is a really nasty piece of work."

"Unlike you, of course!" Silas cackled. "They are looking for their father; they believe that the wild, green man taken from the sea might be him."

"I see," Girth replied. "So now we are hunting for three of them!"

"Yes, and I mean to catch me a fish, Girth!" and he licked his lips in mock delight.

"Quick, we need to find shelter," Fern rose from the bindweed flowers that she was probing and picked up her knapsack.

"Why, what's the problem?" Nathaniel was puzzled. The sky was as blue and cloudless as he had ever seen.

"Look here," Fern pointed to the white flowers of the weed and the old man looked down. "The petals are closing, it's a sure sign of rain approaching."

"She's right," added Hickory, "we should get going."

"Alright, I believe you. I know how you have a feel for these things, it's just hard to think that it could rain on such a beautiful day."

But Fern was right and it wasn't long before the hot and sultry day slipped uneasily into a warm and stormy night. A forceful wind picked up and a clash of black and threatening clouds pounded down thunder on the land, like a battering ram crashing against a castle gate. Far under the storm clouds, the three figures that passed quietly through the wild woods hid from the wrath that now beat down hard upon them.

Even under the canopy of trees, a swirling wind whipped their faces and a cold, heavy rain fell cruelly upon them. They soon realised that they must halt and take safer shelter. They couldn't continue further while the tempest blew, so they stopped underneath a large elm tree, lay upon the wet floor and curled up in the tree's contorted roots. As the thunder came once again they hid their faces under their hoods and tried desperately to sleep.

But Nathaniel couldn't rest and as he opened his eyes to the storm again he blinked in wonder at what he saw. The branches and limbs of the trees were winding themselves around the three of them to create a refuge from the raging storm. Within minutes they disappeared from view, held tightly by the trees and cradled in safety just as the east wind tore through the wood and nature began its battle.

The trees of the wild wood now stood firm, their shield wall unbreakable, valiant, withstanding the pounding onslaught of the storm's army. Again and again the cavalry of the east wind tore across the fields and swarmed down upon the brave defenders of the wood. Slight birch saplings fell bloodied in the wake of the assault. Yet in their stead great oaken warriors stood proudly firm like rocks in the ocean and slender hornbeams twisted and turned avoiding and parrying the thrusts of the east wind's spears.

And then the storm was over. The east wind had admitted defeat and summoned its minions on to fight its next battle. The shattered, embattled, besieged Army of the Wildwood had stood firm and proud and Fern, Hickory and Nathaniel had stayed safe and secure within its tender care.

23: Old Winter

~ Those who live alone, make friends with care ~

After losing a night's travelling time because of the storm, Nathaniel had decided to carry on the journey during the day and by late afternoon, after an exhausting march, the three travellers had left the wild wood far behind.

Though they were tired, they had not gone hungry, for they had feasted on blackcurrants, wild strawberries and berries that Nathaniel had never even seen before, let alone eaten. He watched in awe as Hickory pulled crowberries, snowberries, bilberries and barberries free from torturous heights and thorny hedgerows without a scratch on him. When he tried, he pulled out squashed fruit and an arm pricked with barberry thorns. He howled curses in pain and then found great embarrassment when the children asked him what the new words had meant. So, he gave up and sat back as they seemed to gather fruit from nowhere, "I see why your people can remain hidden in the wild wood," he told them. "What need have you of our world, when you can find food where I see only thorns." Fern and Hickory smiled as they thought of their lost home and then Nathaniel finished the last of his berries and stood up.

"Come on then. We can rest with a friend of mine tonight," he said. "I have sent her warning and she may be able to help us with more than just board and lodging."

"Why? Who is she?" Hickory asked.

"Her name is Old Winter," Nathaniel replied and then he began to recite a poem,

"The bright birds sing and the wind
doth blow,
there's not a thing,
Old Winter doesn't know."

Admittedly, it's her own rhyme, but it has some truth in it. You see, she is what some people call a wise woman or a *seer*, she can tell a little of the future and she is learned in the use of herbs."

"But why is she called Old Winter?" Fern asked. "That seems a strange name, even for your people!"

"From childhood, her hair has been snowy white, as if touched by the frost and that is how she had been given her nickname. All but her family shunned her and as she grew up, and they passed away, she sought the sanctuary of the wood. She became a hermit - an outcast."

"Let us hurry then, for I am scared. I feel that we're being followed though I haven't seen or heard anything," Fern replied anxiously.

"The sooner we are on our way, the better

then," Nathaniel replied and took them both by the hand and led them back out of the trees.

❧❧❧

The tiny hut lay ahead, alone and bleak, shipwrecked in a grasping sea of mud. As they slowly waded across the black field the earth seemed to be pulling them downward to some dark and murky underworld. A slight, crooked figure then emerged from the tumbledown hut. Even from this distance a straggle of white hair was clearly visible through the dying light of the early evening sun.

"It is her!" whispered Nathaniel. "Old Winter."

The dark, huddled figure slowly bent to the ground and brushed away some earth from the plants underneath. From beneath a shawl a small, wrinkled hand searched knowingly in the undergrowth and tugged at its prize. Uprooting the plant, the old woman dropped the slender herb into her basket and renewed her search. Then, she looked up and called out through the half-light, "Nathaniel Drinkstone!" her voice croaked like an old rook. "Come in and bring your friends."

Once inside the tiny hut, they sat upon the floor and blinked through the darkness while the strange old woman muttered and mumbled as she busied herself by the fireside. She brought over bowls of broth for them all. Her voice was hushed and soothing. "Let us not talk now, for you are tired and hungry." They took the broth and ate greedily and then they soon fell asleep amongst the warm fresh reeds by the fireside.

All night they rested and when the first pale light of morning came they awoke early. They sat in silence and ate some dry bread and drank some more broth and when they were fully refreshed the old woman sat with them.

"I am an outcast just like you," she said to the children, her eyes staring in wonder at their green skin, "and yes, I am as old as I look. I have been on this earth for ninety-three years and I have seen much in that time."

"Can you help us?" Fern looked up into the old hermit's eyes pleadingly.

"I do not know my dear," she answered, "though I have much knowledge of the wilds."

"What do you know of our people?" Fern asked longingly.

"I have often heard of the peoples of the woodland," she replied as the children drew closer, "but I have never seen any of them - that is until now," and she smiled down upon them. "What I do know is that there are tidings of despair that reach my tired old ears. The animals and birds tell me, not in words of course, for no-one can speak to them." The children smiled. "But," she continued, "something has happened in the forest realm. There is some fresh danger within the wood which I have not perceived before."

"It is as I feared," Fern stood up and paced the room. "Our homeland is lost, I have seen it in my dreams."

"No!" exclaimed Hickory defiantly. "It cannot be so."

"Wait," Old Winter took Fern's hand firmly in her own, "I must tell you, I have heard strange words in the wind, voices howling warning words, at times even the trees seem to whisper them to me. But I don't know what they mean. Perhaps you can understand them?"

"What are they?" Fern asked the old woman.

"Cai tor malor, Cai tor malor. This is what I hear, over and over."

Fern's face lost all colour and Hickory stood up anxiously.

"You know what the words mean, don't you?" Nathaniel was startled by the children's reaction to Old Winter's words.

"Yes, I know what the words mean," Fern let go of Old Winter's bony hand and turned to face Nathaniel. "You are hunted, you are hunted!"

"That settles it then," Nathaniel rose from

the floor. "If somebody is searching for us we must leave immediately. The sooner we get to Orford, the sooner we can find this green man."

Whilst Nathaniel and Hickory packed their few belongings, Fern and Old Winter fell deep into conversation. They discussed herbs and their properties, the mushrooms and fungi that were useful and the powers of various trees and flowers; in that brief hour the old woman learnt more about herblore than in all her preceding ninety-three years.

When it came time to leave, the old woman gave Nat a small dagger. "You may yet need this Nathaniel. I feel danger nearby."

"But then you will be defenceless," he replied.

"The danger does not follow me. Besides my time is nigh, I have lived long enough upon this earth." She looked at the children and smiled. "I wish you luck my dears," she said as she handed the children a fresh loaf of bread. "Now I can meet my God knowing I have seen all of his creatures."

They thanked her for her help and by the time they reached the bottom of the field and turned to wave goodbye the old hermit had already disappeared back into her tumbledown cottage.

Barely an hour after dusk had fallen and the travellers had said their goodbyes, two flaming torches appeared on the dark horizon. An owl hooted in warning and a hare slipped below ground as heavy hooves thudded to a halt outside the old hermit's cottage.

"Come in," Old Winter's voice croaked from inside the hut, "I have been expecting you!"

Silas of Wickham climbed down from his black horse and pushed the door open. His servant kept vigil outside as the moon broke through the high clouds and shone down its pale light. "Where are they?" Silas shouted his question through the gloom of the cottage.

"Who do you mean?" Old Winter asked back.

"You know who I mean! Tell me now and I will end it quickly for you. Keep me waiting, and I'll burn you as a witch!" Silas' voice grew louder as his frustration rose.

"I won't tell you anything. I've lived my whole life defying the likes of you," Old Winter shouted and as Silas pulled out his thin bladed dagger, she threw the pot of boiling broth at him. The witchfinder yelled as the hot soup splattered over his upraised arms but he pushed home his dagger and a sudden scream of pain came forth from the old woman. Then silence fell upon the desolate hut.

Old Winter lay upon the floor and looked up through the open doorway at the moon. Her long-awaited death had come and she went happily and although pain coursed through her body she closed her eyes and smiled.

Minutes later, Silas left the hut stepping over her limp body. He held a handful of scrolls and put them hurriedly in his saddlebag. Then he took his torch from Girth's hand and touched the scarlet flame to the wooden hut. The soft breeze fanned the fire and the hut went up in a blaze of red and gold.

Silas climbed onto his horse and swore out loud. He had lost the scent of his prey and he was angry. "We will away to Wickham Manor and take rest Girth."

"Yes Sire," Girth dutifully replied.

"From there we can renew the hunt. They will not slip away from us again." And as swiftly as they had come, they disappeared back over the dark horizon as Old Winter's hut tumbled to the floor in a cloud of smoke.

24: The Gooseberry Fair

~ Ripe berries are the treasures of the hedgerow ~

A gentle tapping echoed through the morning air as the thin frame of Nathaniel Drinkstone was bent in labour by the arched entrance to the chancel of St. Mary's church, Grundisburgh. Carefully his chisel bit away at the sandstone and slowly a delicate face gradually appeared in the archway. Hiding behind three huge fern leaves, the eyes and nose of a green man peered down from above. Within minutes he was finished and pleased with his hurried labours, the old man quickly collected his tools together and slid them into his knapsack. Now, there were carvings all along the trail they had taken. Faces appeared in churches from Walsham-le-Willows, Thurston, Woolpit, Tostock, and now to Grundisburgh.

Just as he was tidying away however, he heard the mumblings of the priest echo down the path outside. As the church door opened, Nathaniel threw himself onto the floor of the chancel and hid behind the altar. As the priest walked down the nave, Nathaniel thought up a plausible story to tell, but luckily it wasn't needed. The priest turned away and strode over to the small door that led up to the bell tower. As he disappeared from view the old man ran out of the church and slipped back into the trees to find the children.

A warm morning sun smiled down upon the three travellers and the few clouds that dotted the blue sky danced high and harmlessly far above them. Underneath their weary feet, the ground now started to roll slowly downward towards the coastal plain. They followed the valley floor for a mile or two and then suddenly, quite unexpectedly, they heard voices. The children slipped out of sight behind a hedgerow before Nathaniel had even turned to warn them and he quickly followed suit.

Bouncing merrily along the pathway came a procession of a dozen or so villagers who held aloft a great pole. Upon it was a dummy dressed in leaves and a crown made from gooseberries was perched precariously upon its head. The marching villagers were similarly decorated with painted faces and leaf-strewn tunics and the children looked on in astonishment. They instinctively wanted to run out to greet the procession, but Nathaniel held them back.

"No children," he answered their questioning eyes, "they are not your folk. It's just a parade. They are probably going to Wickham

Market. There must be some local fair taking place."

"Can we follow them?" asked Hickory excitedly.

"Oh yes! Please, Nathaniel!" begged Fern.

Nathaniel stroked his beard and pondered for a long moment. "Alright," he finally concluded. "We'll go into Wickham Market and visit the fair. If all the townsfolk are dressed as these, we will have no need for a disguise. In fact, I will be the only one who will stand out!"

He laughed and the children laughed with him. It had been an anxious couple of days and the fair would be a welcome relief. Nathaniel had begun to feel his age and although he had eaten well enough on the journey, the thought of a few tasty morsels from the fair was a welcome one indeed. Before long he had his own crown of leaves and a face smeared with berry juice and he led the children down to the town and their very first visit to a fair.

Wickham Market was a thriving town, where traders from the coast met with rich merchants from the wool towns of Lavenham and Melford. The inhabitants of the town had fed off these meetings like vultures and they too had become rich and prosperous. But with this wealth had come a certain pride and arrogance.

There was no doubt that their town was beautiful though. The market square, with its cobbled stones, dredged up from the shores at Aldeburgh, sparkled like ice, as the dawn rose. And the houses that stood neatly around the square were just as entrancing. Their timbers were carved in the shapes of fabulous beasts and mythical figures and between the wood, the plasterwork was painted in bright colours. Woolpit's cottages were homely and cosy but they were also dark and dull in comparison with these. As the children stared at them in awe, Nathaniel told them how the deep pink colour was made from the roots of the madder plant; that the red-brown shade was called cinnabar and that the orpiment yellow was made from the poison arsenic.

In the centre row of houses, the Manor House of Wickham Market stood tallest and brightest of all. A small wooded balcony jutted out from the front and above the great oaken door a beautiful stained glass window glimmered in the morning sun. Fern felt herself drawn toward the scene upon the glass. It seemed to be an old woman hanging from a tree but Nathaniel quickly took her by the arm and led her into the square where the festivities were already well under way.

The voices and sounds of the celebration nearly suffocated the children who almost drowned in a sea of cheering, laughing and merrymaking. The smells of the stalls overwhelmed their delicate senses and they stared longingly at tables with toffee apples, honeycakes, cheese curd pastries and summer fruit pies. They watched in wonder at the fancy costumes, the puppet shows, the fire-breathers and the jugglers. But the children hurried past the pig-roast and the stalls with the boiled geese and the fresh sausages hanging by the dozen, while Nathaniel looked on hungrily and licked his lips.

Then, they all stared carefully into the centre of the square as two great hulking men wrestled each other to the floor while a number of sour faced townsfolk took bets, shouted, jeered and spat upon the two fighters.

It wasn't just men that were fighting either. There were cockerels attacking each other in one corner and a pack of dogs were tied up in another, ready to do battle with some as yet unknown opponent but the children shied away from these events and hurried over to look once again upon the dummy of the Gooseberry King.

Townsfolk and villagers from all around had flocked here to buy and sell goods, to be entertained, to get drunk and to eat their fill all in praise of the harvest of the humble gooseberry.

Each year one village had the honour of making the Gooseberry King and this year the tiny hamlet of Hasketon had been chosen and all twelve of its inhabitants had come along today. Many others there had dressed for the occasion too, from the smallest concession of a green crown to elaborate costumes in the shape of gooseberries and green dresses covered in leaves. As Fern and Hickory looked around them they began to feel quite at home.

Then, quite suddenly, a piercing shriek of pain shuddered through the jovial air and a deep growling noise followed close behind it. Some beast was angry, that much was clear. Nathaniel looked across to the far corner of the market square. He already knew what he would find there and the sight of it still sickened him. He quickly tried to divert the children's attention from the violent scene and hurriedly pointed out a man walking on stilts but the children had been already drawn to the sounds of the wounded animal. Before he could stop them, Fern and Hickory broke free and ran to the corner. They stood in horror at the back of a watching crowd as a pack of half a dozen barking dogs jumped back and forth at a bear like violent waves crashing upon a beach.

The black bear was enormous and it growled in anger but it was chained by the ankle to a great post and its claws had been cruelly clipped. Rivulets of blood already ran down its hindquarters and although one dog lay injured on the ground, the others bit and slashed at the bear in a frenzied attack. The children instantly felt great affinity to this creature of the forest and they knew they had to try and do something, anything to stop this cruelty, but as they moved forward a gentle but firm hand held them back.

"No," whispered Nathaniel, "not now."

As he spoke, the crowd around the bear baiting drew away anyway and the dogs were tied up again and all eyes now turned upward to the small balcony of the Manor House in the centre of the square. The mood of the fair darkened, a feeling of foreboding cast a great shadow over everything. Then, underneath a head of long, lank black hair a thin, angular face peered down upon the throng of merry-makers and a hush reverberated around the square and Nathaniel turned as a stallholder behind him whispered to his wife, "What does Silas want now?"

The figure on the balcony spoke with a quiet, menacing voice, "I am sorry to interrupt the festivities but I need the assistance of you good people. I am, as ever, searching for those evil servants of the devil . . . witches." He spat the final word out with relish. "These ones are particularly strange," he continued, "for they are . . . green!"

The crowd started to mutter but Silas stopped their chatter with a raised hand. "I am looking for a boy and girl and I believe they have come this way, for they are heading to the coast. If any of you have seen anyone strange or suspicious then you must tell me immediately - you will be well rewarded."

Nathaniel and the children froze in terror, realising that, quite unwittingly, they had walked straight into the arms of their hunters. Seeing the danger, the old man pulled the children close to him and in a whisper told them to edge their way to the far end of the square. He was unaware however of the suspicious gaze of a toothless old woman who stood close to them.

"What do these devils look like, my Lord?" a gruff voice shouted out from the crowd.

"Well, I have not actually seen them, but I'm told they are pale green in colour with hair that is almost white," Silas answered.

"How many are there?" the old woman clucked as her eyes met Nathaniel's.

A large, dark, bearded man moved out from the shadows behind Silas and spoke out loudly. "Two children and they are travelling with one old man. He may be a witch too!" answered Girth Harthblood, Silas' henchman.

The withered old crone suddenly raised her

staff accusingly at Nathaniel just at the same moment as a small podgy boy pointed a stubby finger directly at Hickory. The hulking figure of Girth saw the commotion, bent close and whispered into Silas' ear. From the balcony of the Manor House, Silas of Wickham's voice then shrieked out, "They are here among us! Get them!"

Screams of terror, cries of outrage and roars of hatred filled the air as the townspeople of Wickham Market turned upon the three strangers. Hands grasped towards them and the old woman clasped Nathaniel as he and the children tried to escape!

Fern somehow managed to evade the outstretched hands and moved almost unseen through the crowd, like a green ghost. Silently, she slipped through the townsfolk and hurriedly made for the far corner of the square.

Hickory ran too. His speed was astonishing! He twisted and dodged the arms and hands that grabbed at him and just when it looked like he was trapped, he dived onto the cobbled ground and rolled under a market stall. Before the fishmonger could do anything, Hickory had kicked at the stall's legs and the fresh fish fell clattering to the ground in front of the onrushing crowd. Men, women, youths and youngsters all tripped and fell on the slippery fare.

As more townspeople came upon him,
Hickory picked himself up from the ground and
jumped onto a stall full of fresh summer fruit.
Then he dived headlong into the air and
somersaulted over the flailing arms of the
stallholder.

Meanwhile, Fern had slipped off a small
leather bag from her belt and had run to where the
baited bear sat slumped upon the ground licking
its wounds. While mayhem followed Hickory in
the centre of the square, Fern had for the time
being escaped. She knelt down by the bear, took
some leaves from her pouch and proceeded to rub
them on the bear's ankle while she whispered
gently into its ear.

Nathaniel had finally broken free of the
scratching grip of the old woman and had turned
round to help Hickory who had just been knocked
to the floor by the large figure of Girth Harthblood.
Four or five pairs of hands now bore down upon
the terrified boy. From the back of the group Silas
loomed down from the shadows like some great
bat and then hands fell upon Nathaniel too! In
seconds the baying crowd would have their
'devils' and a hanging would surely ensue.

But then, a great roar echoed through the
town of Wickham Market. Fern had set the bear
free and now he tore into the square, rose to his
full height of eight feet and towered above them

all. He was huge!

The dogs turned and barked viciously but the bear was no longer tied down and they stood no chance. As the first dog was let loose to attack him, the bear smashed a great paw down upon it and the dog fell whimpering to the floor. Another was despatched the same way and yet a third hauled out of the beast's path. Finally, the remaining dogs slunk away defeated and the bear turned towards the townsfolk.

As it lumbered through the fair it pushed over stalls and swiped at the fleeing crowds. The creature's owner tried in vain to whip the beast into submission but the bear caught hold of the whip and pulled its master to the ground. The man hit his head upon the cobbles and fell unconscious.

The group of men that now held Nathaniel and Hickory pinioned to the floor were caught in two minds. If they ran they would lose their 'witches' and their reward but if they stayed put they might lose their heads.

One by one the imprisoning hands slipped from Nathaniel and Hickory as the men lost their courage. Finally only Silas, Girth and one other man held onto them. The bear now stood right above them and with lightning speed it bent down and literally hoisted the townsman above its head. It turned and threw him down upon the ground next to the broken fish stall, with a terrifying crack of bones.

The beast turned back to the others that now looked up into its black eyes with terror and then it fell down upon them. At the last moment Girth let go of Nathaniel and he struggled free. Silas had the boy, but now the bear had Silas! It yanked him up by his silken robes but the fine thread ripped and he was able to break free but not before the bear had slashed at his throat. If the beast's claws had not been clipped it would have been the end for him. Instead, the witchfinder stumbled to the ground gasping for air and Girth pulled him to safety, just in time.

During this chaos, Fern had hidden under the shadow of the roof of the great granary barn that stood in the eastern corner of the square. Now she moved out into the sunlight and shouted to Nathaniel and Hickory. "Quickly, this way while there is still a chance of escape!" The bear now roared in triumph as it roamed around an emptying market square. Nat and Hickory jumped to their feet and ran to where Fern stood. "Well, they won't forget this Gooseberry Fair in a hurry," laughed Nathaniel.

And with that they ran past the great barn, rose steadily into the fields that surrounded the town and slipped quietly into a sea of high grasses. Their shoulders and then their heads slipped beneath the green waves and they fell from sight.

Minutes later they re-appeared from the depths and climbed up a rolling hillside. They were about a mile or so away from the town now but even from here they could hear the growling voice of the bear - the new Lord of Wickham Market, the Master of the Gooseberry Fair.

25: Rendel's Forest

~ Forest flowers have hidden powers ~

Within minutes of losing their 'witches', Silas and Girth had mounted their steeds and taken up the chase. They rode south out of Wickham Market and slipped across the river Deben at Uffas' Ford. They had not seen where their prey had gone but they knew they were heading for Orford and they were sure it wouldn't take long to pick up their trail, so they entered Rendel's Forest with a feeling of expectancy.

Ahead of the hunters, Nathaniel, Fern and Hickory trod quietly through the same forest as a squirrel darted across the woodland floor and scampered up a broad limbed ash tree. High up in the canopy of the ancient woodland, nesting hawfinches chattered away and as a green woodpecker tapped out his familiar song, sunlight glittered silver-white on the bark of a tall, slender birch tree, its delicate leaves shimmering like a knight's mail coat on the soft wind. Ox-eye daisies danced gaily around their feet and towers of willowherb rose above the undergrowth of ferns and nettles. Softly, a fallow deer tiptoed past them and the two green children felt at one with their surroundings.

But for the witchfinders behind them, this was a strange and mysterious world where the bewildering song of the trees lured them further and further away from their prey. Eventually, they were forced to leave their horses behind and struggle forward on foot but every way they went, tree trunks seemed to have fallen in their way, branches entangled them, roots tripped them and gripped them and great ferns beat harshly across their faces. It seemed as if the forest itself hampered their path at every turn.

Girth Harthblood, the witchfinder's accomplice, was of Viking descent and although it had been nearly three hundred years since his ancestors had sailed up the inlet of the East Coast, their bloodlust and heathen ways ran strongly in his veins. He was finding the pursuit through this unwelcome wood heavy going indeed and found his height and frame were not suited to the tangled paths of the forest. As the nettles threw themselves stinging upon his legs like swarms of bees and as the willowy branches of elm sprang back in his face like a master's whip, his temper rose.

Despite the delaying actions of the wood, it hadn't stopped the two men from making ground on the weary travellers. Nathaniel had slowed right down whilst the children had become lost in thought as they passed merrily through familiar surroundings. It wasn't long before Silas glimpsed sight of the old man through the dappled light of the forest. "They are just ahead," he whispered furtively to Girth. He couldn't make out the shapes of the children because they were too well hidden within their own domain but he knew they were there, for he could hear the girl softly singing.

Quickly, the witchfinders unsheathed their swords and made ready to take their prey, but seconds before they would have caught them, Girth slashed a limb from a willow tree that stood defiantly in his way and the children felt the tree cry out. As they turned, they saw the black figures running towards them. "Run!" Fern's scream shattered the silence and quickly awoke Nathaniel from his daydream.

Hickory immediately took to his heels, skipped over a fallen tree trunk and slipped out of sight into a dense patch of bramble. Fern too ran swiftly and was almost out of reach when she felt something slip over her head. With a violent jolt she was pulled to the floor. A rope was round her neck and as she was turned backward she saw the grinning face of Silas of Wickham behind her.

"Now I have you," he squealed in delight and his black eyes sparkled out gleefully from his pale face as he pulled the rope taut.

Nathaniel had seen what had happened and

hastily pulled Old Winter's knife from his belt and slashed down at the rope that held Fern like an unbroken horse. The blow was not enough to cut through the thick cord however and as he pulled up his arm to strike it again Girth stumbled through the undergrowth and knocked him to the ground with his shoulder.

Nathaniel fell heavily at the base of an elm tree and looked upward helplessly at the bearded hulk above him. Girth turned his heavy body, pulling his full bulk around and smashed the flat edge of his sword downward just missing Nathaniel's ear. The trunk of the elm tree cracked open and then the old man rolled over just in time to avoid Girth's second hammer blow.

Suddenly, a voice could be heard through the trees, somebody or something was coming to their aid. The voice called out again but Nathaniel did not understand the words for it was in a strange tongue, but Fern looked up in recognition. Then the caller came into view. It was Hickory, but he wasn't alone. Two large beasts followed close behind him.

Girth had by now crunched a heavy boot upon Nathaniel's chest and the old man was pinned to the forest floor. Silas was slowly, but surely, pulling Fern toward him and he now clasped the handle of a long-bladed dagger in his left hand.

But then the beasts behind Hickory passed out of the shadows and all could see them clearly. They were huge stags and they thumped their hooves heavily upon the forest floor in fury. Looking coldly at the men, they put down their great antlers and charged.

Silas immediately let go of the rope that held Fern and clumsily struggled to pull his dagger free. Fern pulled the noose off from around her neck and ran to Hickory. As the first stag crashed into the witchfinder he swung his dagger blindly, caught his blade in the animal's horns and watched helplessly as it was sent spinning to the floor. Fearfully he backed away from the stag but the beast came on and Silas called out to Girth for help.

But the witchfinder's assistant was also locked in a duel, though he still had his blade and he swung his great sword with power and prowess. The stag recoiled before him as his ferocious strokes whirled. Then with an almighty crash Girth cut deep into the stag's antlers and the animal gave out a despairing cry. Now he smelt blood and he beat the stag backwards until it could no longer butt him. Instead the animal turned away and with his final thrust Girth slashed at its side and a gash opened up on the stag's hindquarters. It limped away in agony as Girth now turned his attention to the plight of his master. But the stag that now stood above the cowering witchfinder had seen its companion limp away and it too now turned and made its escape.

Silas breathed a heavy sigh of relief, but as Girth helped him to his feet the witchfinder swore out loudly, "Damn them!" he cried, as he glanced around the clearing and found all trace of the green children gone! Then, this anger at the way the forest and its beasts had confounded him burst forth like a great wave and he suddenly knew how to destroy them all. "I'll burn you out!" he howled as he pulled a tinderbox from his cloak.

Moments later, a dragon's breath of flame leapt from the burning torch in Silas' outstretched hand and swiftly caught light in the dense undergrowth.

As Fern and Hickory tended to the injured stag they saw the flicker of fire through the trees behind them and screamed a terrifying cry that was echoed by the very trees themselves. Even Nathaniel could feel the horror all around him as the birches, hornbeams and oaks seemed to shriek out in fear. But there was nothing they could do to halt the fire. They ran and ran as the flames burnt quickly through the forest and only when they had reached safety did Nathaniel stop them, as he fell down breathless upon the floor.

"I must rest children," he gasped. "I fear I have spent too many years sat comfortably in my chamber reading books."

"What shall we do then?" Hickory asked in dismay.

"We must leave this forest and make for the road," said Nathaniel.

"No! We will be caught out in the open," Fern did not want to leave the shelter of the trees again.

"I know the risks young lady!" Nathaniel's voice was stern; a strain of tiredness and fear ran through it. "Besides," he continued, "I wouldn't have taken us any further anyway, Wickham is not the only evil thing in this land and we mustn't go any deeper into this wood."

"Why not?" the children asked in unison.

Nathaniel's voice became hushed and then he quietly sang, "Wicked, is the night, that darkens the sky. Evil are the clouds that ride on high. Then, will come the Wyvern-King."

"What's that?" asked Hickory.

"It's from an old song," he replied, "for it is said that there is a Wyvern in the depths of Rendel's Forest".

"A what?" asked Fern.

"As the old Norse poems tell, it is a fire-breather, a man-gobbler, a claw-fighter and a skull-splitter."

The children gathered in close, their eyes widening in wonder.

"A Wyvern, my young friends, if you haven't guessed already, is a two legged serpent . . . or dragon."

The children's faces were furrowed in fear and yet they wanted to know more of this strange creature. "Tell us about it," Hickory pleaded.

"Well, sit down by me, whilst I gain my breath, and I will tell you the tale of King Rendel, though it obviously must be brief, the legend is very long and I cannot relay all of it now." Nathaniel sat upon the mossy grass under a spreading oak and the children sat before him. Quickly he told them the tale of King Rendel.

"King Rendel was the last pagan king of East Anglia. His people were known as the Wyvernfolk. It was said that the prows of their long ships were carved in the shapes of dragons and when they went into battle the wood transformed and the prows came to life. The dragons or Wyverns breathed fire and walked on two legs and they fought alongside Rendel's warriors. They were fearsome and terrifying and no one could stand against them and eventually Rendel carved out a great kingdom in these parts.

But as the King grew old, inevitably his sons began to quarrel over which of them should inherit the throne. One son, Hala, rose up in rebellion against the king. He allied himself with Rendel's greatest enemy King Ethgar of Mercia.

Together, Hala and Ethgar defeated Rendel in a bloody battle right here amongst the trees of the forest. King Rendel was slain, as was Hala and so it was that the cruel Ethgar won the day. He was a merciless man and he put all the Wyvernfolk to the sword, even those that had joined with him in rebellion."

Hickory looked up transfixed, his eyes glued to the old man, for the tales of great battles intrigued and delighted him. "Why did the Wyverns not help Rendel defeat his enemies?" he asked.

"He was ambushed, caught unawares, his army were sleeping and they were here in this forest, far from their ships and the Wyverns did not come to his aid."

"Then what happened?" Hickory asked eagerly.

"A small band of warriors survived the slaughter and hauled up Rendel's ship from the Deben. The great King's body was lain inside with all his treasures and then it was buried under a great mound of earth right in the centre of his forest. The legend says that just as the ship was covered with the first sods of earth, the prow of the King's ship itself came to life. The King's Wyvern is honour-bound to repay his oath and so he stands guard over the King's tomb, even to this day."

"So this creature is alive in this wood?" Fern asked dispassionately. Tales of ancient battles and bloodshed did not inspire wonder in her like it did with her brother, she did not daydream of running headlong into battle clutching a sword or holding firm in the shieldwall, she thought more practically and stared at Nathaniel with thoughts only of how to overcome their current dilemma.

"I will speak with this Wyvern," she stated matter-of-factly.

"Don't be so foolish girl," Nathaniel dismissed the idea immediately. Then, behind them the witchfinder's voice could be heard afresh and they knew they had to act quickly.

"It's not foolish, it is the only way!" Fern's voice was calm and steadfast.

Nathaniel looked thoughtfully into the eyes of the green girl and he knew she was right.

❧

Fern trod gently, almost invisibly, into the heart of the wood and into the blackest, black of Rendel's forest. As something stirred nearby, the wind seemed to whisper a warning, but she carried on. She neither saw nor heard any other creature; nothing else dared approach the Wyvern's lair.

Suddenly, her boot caught in the twisted

brambles under her left foot. She knelt down to
loosen her ankle and felt something firm under her
toes. She placed her fingers around the object; it
was hard and round. Then she pulled it up and
wiped off the layers of earth that clung to it. She
peeled away the last clump of dirt and then drew
backwards, gasping out, as the black eyeless
sockets of a skull stared back at her.

She dropped the lifeless head immediately,
put away the fear from her mind and carried
onwards. At last she came to a mound of grass
and she knew that this had to be King Rendel's
tomb. And then she felt the Wyvern's presence.
It was there, ahead of her, waiting, waiting for its
prey. She panicked - What if she couldn't talk to
it? What if it just attacked? Was it all to end
here? Her hands tingled in anticipation and the
veins on her arms hardened with anxiety. Then,
all around her, the trees shook and she knew it
was too late, she knew it was coming - the
Wyvern was coming!

26: The Wyvern

~ Not all that is dark, is evil ~

There before her it towered, unmoving, unflinching in the shadows of the half-light. At first sight, Fern thought it wasn't actually real at all; it stood so motionless, as if still carved from oak. Was it really just a legend, a creature from a long forgotten tale? But then, as she entered its line of vision, the great beast turned its head and it looked down, directly at her.

She stared right back at the great dragon and studied it carefully. She saw how the Wyvern's face and body were etched with the lines of the wood-grain from which it had once been carved. She glanced at the sharp claws and the spiked tail that curled behind it. She glimpsed the red tongue that flickered like a snake's behind enormous ivory teeth and she gaped at the vast wings that fell from its back. Inside her heart beat wildly, as she sensed the immense power that lay within this ancient creature.

As Fern moved closer, she felt its warm breath upon her face and her nostrils filled with the smell of acrid smoke and rotten flesh, and she then knew that around her feet lay the bones and carcasses of the Wyvern's victims. She shuddered with fear, closed her eyes and in her own gentle language she spoke to the great beast. " Cas mal tuvali," the words fluttered in the air like spiralling leaves on a windy day. But the beast did not reply.

For a split second, after her plea for help, Fern panicked. Was the beast too ancient to understand her? It was after all far older than the trees, birds and animals. Was it about to turn upon her, open its great jaws and devour her whole? Then a flicker of comprehension glinted in the Wyvern's black eyes. It looked deep into Fern's soul and though it did not actually speak to her, she instantly knew what it was thinking.

Quickly, she turned to leave King Rendel's grassy tomb and her light steps were echoed by the heavy thud of the Wyvern's taloned feet. It was following her!

⁂

The Wyvern's claws glinted like warriors' spears and its eyes glowed an incandescent red through the grove as it waited silently for its victims. Nearby, in its shadow, a faint smile appeared on Nathaniel Drinkstone's lips as he thought how ironic it was that this creature of darkness was now defending them against the evil of Silas of Wickham - flame against flame!

Then, as planned, he called out loudly to

Fern and she answered him with a raised voice luring the witchfinders on, like fishermen casting their bait. As the flaming torch that Wickham held came ever closer, the chase reached its climax and suddenly the pursuers crashed down upon the arbor where they expected to find their quarry. But, in an instant, the cries of attack turned swiftly to those of panic and terror. The trap had been sprung!

The Wyvern had lain in wait for long enough, its great claws smashed through the undergrowth as it reached out for the witchfinders, its body rose from the earth on to its great clawed feet like a volcano erupting. In an instant it roared out, its head towering above the two shaken men. A flash of scorching breath bit through the heavy air and a crunch of talons echoed in the night as the beast bore down upon them.

Nathaniel and the children could see little through the dense foliage and even though they knew they should take flight, they were rooted to the spot, keen to see the outcome of this encounter. Then, they saw the great beast raise its serpent's tail and swing it around like a huge spiked club.

Girth, his sword drawn and holding a small leather buckler shield, took the full brunt of the Wyvern's first thrust. The weight and force of the

tail battered down upon him like a blacksmith's
hammer crashing upon an anvil. It knocked him
flying to the ground. His head glanced off the
knotted roots of an elm tree and his body
thumped to the forest floor.

He gave out a muffled groan as he slowly
rose up again but it was too late. The Wyvern
had moved in for the kill. A bright, golden flame
spewed forth from the monster's mouth. The fiery
breath set light to his beard and hair. Suddenly,
he was lit up like a torch and he cried out in
agony. Then the Wyvern's right claw crashed
down upon the dazed warrior, his body fell limp
and he fell, never to rise to battle again.

But this was no battle, the Wyvern was
wholly in command and now it turned upon Silas,
who cowered, sword in hand, trembling behind a
tall beech tree. It looked as if nothing could save
the witchfinder now. But then the Wyvern itself
cried out in agony, for Silas' fire that had been
burning fast through the ancient woodland had
now encircled them. In a burst of golden flames it
engulfed the Wyvern and the witchfinder. Silas
screamed as the blaze took hold of his long, black
cloak and wrestled him to the ground.

The Wyvern too, was trapped and the
wooden beast caught light swiftly. Bright flames
ran along its wings, red talons of fire gripped its
great body and pulled it to the floor and a

mournful cry rocked the forest to its roots as it finally fell. The mighty Wyvern's long vigil over the tomb of King Rendel had come to a fiery end.

As Nathaniel and the children cleared the edge of Rendel's forest they heard that cry and knew that the beast had perished. Fern stopped dead in her tracks, turned and gazed back at the burning woods. She whispered a silent prayer as trees crashed to the floor behind her. Then, she followed the others and ran towards the flat marshes ahead of her.

If she had lingered a few minutes longer she would have seen a thin, burning figure crawl out from the flaming claws of Rendel's Forest. It rolled in the long grasses and its cloak of fire was extinguished. It coughed, choked and spluttered as it gulped in mouthfuls of the salty air that blew inland from the coast. And then it rose to its feet and its black eyes looked to the marshes ahead . . . Silas of Wickham was still alive!

27: The Butley Ferry

~ The rivers are the children of the sea ~

A soft, salty summer breeze whistled through the tall fox-tail grasses that covered the landscape to the far horizon as a marsh harrier rose majestically above the flat reedbeds and then swooped down to the waters below. Almost hidden beneath the bog-rushes and the reeds lay meandering streams, hidden inlets and muddy creeks which criss-crossed the land like veins across an old man's hands. And beyond all that was the wide Butley river with its clear, cold waters and its ancient oysterbeds.

This was a strange and inhospitable world to the green children. There were few trees here. Instead there were wide, sweeping spaces, and flat stretches of plain that lay open to the elements. Under a wide, clear, penetrating blue sky they felt small and exposed and it seemed as if the gulls that flew squawking overhead might themselves swoop down and pick them off like crabs on the shore.

Yet Nathaniel was there, and his resolve stood firm. He pushed them on, though they were weary beyond belief, but the old man knew that their goal was almost in reach now. A few more miles and the cylindrical stone keep of Orford

Castle would rise into view.

❧❧❧

As they approached the river they heard distant voices over the bank and quickly threw themselves behind a clump of tall grasses. Silently, they looked down upon the wide, flat river and stared thoughtfully at the stick-like figure that skilfully worked the Butley Ferry. The wizened old ferryman they spied upon led a horse and cart onto his raft and then he held aloft his punting pole. With a timeless movement he pushed the pole down to the riverbed and smoothly the ferry moved away from the bank. Then the ferryman pulled the pole up above his head and deftly let it slip down through his fingers again and back into the grey waters. He repeated this action like clockwork until the ferry had crossed to the far side of the river.

"Well, there are no trees to help us across the river here," Nathaniel whispered and the children smiled as they remembered the old man's last river crossing. "Yet we must cross somehow and this appears to be the only way." He pointed down to the ferryman as the horse and cart trundled off the raft and drove away along the dry track and disappeared behind the dunes.

"But we will be recognised," Fern stated.

"Yes I know," Nathaniel replied, "and no

doubt the ferryman will inform all of his passengers of our passing. But I don't see what other option we have."

They watched glumly as the ferryman pushed his punt into the water and made his way back again to their side of the river. "Wait a moment!" Hickory exclaimed. "Look at what I can see."

Just then another cart, pulled by two fat oxen creaked into view. Driving it, was a ruddy-faced villager singing a bawdy song as he directed his cart towards the ferry. But it was the freshly harvested crop in the back of the cart that had gained Hickory's attention. It was full of beans - green beans!

Understanding instantly what the boy intended, Nathaniel broke from their hiding place, called down to the singing driver and engaged him in conversation. Whilst the carter was kept busy, the children scampered out from behind the clump of grasses and down to the back of the cart. Quickly, they climbed inside and hid themselves under the beans.

Peering out from underneath the vegetables the children stared up at the blue sky and made shapes in their heads from the dancing white clouds above them. Before long they heard voices and then they felt the cart trundle onto the ferry.

Minutes later they felt it bump off again

onto the far shore and heard Nathaniel's voice loudly exclaim his thanks to the driver for taking him 'all the way to Orford.' The children gripped hands through the beans in excitement and settled down for the journey ahead. A journey they hoped would take them at last to their father.

28: The Wild Man

~ The creatures of the sea are wild and free ~

The dungeon was cold, wet and miserable and the stench that rose from it was awful. In the far recesses was the hole that was nicknamed *'no mercy'*, where prisoners could neither sit down nor stand up straight. It was here, in this godforsaken place that the lone prisoner of Orford Castle was presently kept. Through the darkness a single shaft of light slipped through the iron grill of the trapdoor and shone upon the lonely, mournful face of the captive. Hanging from his shackled feet the wild man of the sea was a beaten and desolate figure, denied his freedom and left to suffer in this dark silence, deep below ground.

Then, the gloom was broken. A key turned, the door opened and the guards cut loose the prisoner. They walked him slowly across to the doorway and as he moved he stumbled and fell. In the water, he had been as elegant and graceful as a dolphin, but on ground the creature was as clumsy as a blind man. "You have a visitor," the guard laughed as he grabbed hold of his leathery skin and brought him upright. As he looked up to the light the wild man grinned through teeth as crooked as a broken fence. "I wouldn't smile if I

were you," the guard continued, "your visitor is the constable and he's come to inspect you!"

❦

Bartholomew de Glanville was a tall, elegant man who spoke with the authority of a Norman Lord and the power of the King's command and he stared coldly at the prisoner before him. "Where was he found?"

"Two fishermen pulled him out of Hollesley Bay, Sire. He was caught up in their nets."

"Does he speak?"

"No Sire, not a single murmur has come from his lips."

De Glanville reached down to the elaborate scabbard that hung from his belt and unsheathed his sword. With a flick of his hand the blade licked the wild man's forearm and the creature cried out in agony. "He does have a tongue then," de Glanville mocked, "hidden behind those ragged teeth."

The wild man's eyes lit up with fury and he struck out at the constable. But his assault was in vain. The chains, bound tightly around his wrists, were gripped hard by the guards and though he possessed a great strength he could not overpower the firm grip upon him. De Glanville slowly removed his fingers from his ermine gauntlet and viciously struck his captive across

181

the face with the back of his hand.

"Insolent wretch! Throw him back into the cell!" With a glance of hatred de Glanville turned on his heels and left the grim, dark dungeon.

It was just after dusk when the cart full of beans rattled onto the cobbled market square of the small port of Orford. All through the journey the lonely song of the gulls had lulled the travellers closer and closer to the sea and at last they had arrived at their journey's end.

Hidden by the fading light, the children slipped down from the back of the cart and ran to meet Nathaniel. As the moon rose silently in the eastern sky the old man and the children stood quietly and surveyed the scene around them.

They saw a cluster of cottages surrounding the square and narrow streets leading down to the quay. There was an inn with a large sign that creaked softly in the wet wind and the outline of a church could be seen, just behind it. But all of this, from the marketplace down to the cusp of the harbour, lay in the shadow of the great castle.

Nathaniel pointed up to the stone fortress. "Well! There it is," he stated matter of factly. "Let's take a closer look."

"It's wonderful!" Hickory was transfixed by the grandeur and power of the stone giant that towered above him. Never before had he seen anything like it.

"It may be wonderful young Hickory," Nathaniel replied earnestly, "but how on earth do we get inside it?"

"We can't!" gasped Fern. From the cover of the copse of trees they all stared up again at the mighty stronghold of Orford Castle and each of them knew the impossibility of the task ahead.

Before them lay three rings of ditches and ramparts and a great circle of sharpened stakes stuck out from the outer ring like a row of dragon's teeth. Beyond this network of earth defences there stood the outer curtain wall. It was about twenty feet tall and was broken up into sections, which were commanded by a pair of towers that projected forward into the field. In the centre of the curtain wall stood a large gateway, which had opened up like a huge mouth for a line of mail-clad soldiers to pass into.

Behind the curtain wall, on a dominating mound, the cylindrical keep of the castle rose a hundred feet into the air. It stood tall and proud and the black arrow slits flickered with red fire like watchful eyes. Three towers projected out from corners of the keep and a thin line of smoke rose high into the darkening night.

Then, as if their plight could not get any worse, a biting cold wind blew off the North Sea and brought a chill rain down upon them. Within moments the castle disappeared behind a grey mist and the three hooded figures were forced to draw away from their watching place. Autumn had announced its arrival and the Castle of Orford seemed more impregnable than ever.

29: The Singer of Songs
~ Trusting a stranger is like walking on ice ~

Down by the harbourside, the clatter and bustle of the end of the day rang out across Orford quay. The noise drifted on up through the narrow streets of the town and swirled away towards the castle. As a silent sea mist blew in, an endless array of fisherfolk, merchantmen, foreign traders and sea-weary sailors packed up their wares and drew in their sails. Three hooded strangers were also there and hidden by the grey blanket of fog, they asked endless questions about the wild green man and the defences of the castle. But their search for help was fruitless.

As darkness descended the strangers turned down a narrow alleyway and saw a small crowd gathered around a tall, spindly figure. The fellow at the centre of all this attention wore a long cloak about him and in the torchlight of the street it shimmered in brightly coloured quarters. Under an odd shaped felt hat they saw a long, pale face with sparkling blue eyes and out from his angular chin stuck a tuft of red hair.

Whilst they approached him he put away some juggling balls into a large leather bag and then from its seemingly endless bottom he pulled out a coin and three cups. He placed the coin under one of the cups and set up his game upon the end of an upturned beer barrel. Nathaniel and the children couldn't take their eyes off the gawky figure and they felt themselves pulled in toward him, unable to drag themselves away from his spellbinding presence. They watched carefully as the curious figure then proceeded to trick and deceive the gullible crowd around him moving the three cups with lightning speed.

The local fishermen and sailors rapidly lost all their own money and the crowd slowly drew away, so Hickory moved forward. "Do it again," he asked the strange character.

"Certainly, young man," replied the odd fellow, and his words seemed to dance along the narrow street, jumping and skipping as he spoke.

He put the coin back under the middle cup and then moved them about the barrel end at a lightning pace. It was far too quick for Nathaniel to see which one had the coin under it but Hickory just smiled beneath his hood and pointed to the cup on the left hand side. The curious man laughed and lifted it up. Underneath, was the coin and he picked it up and handed it to Hickory.

"Well done, no-one has ever done that before but then I have never met anyone like you before!"

"What do you mean by that?" Nathaniel

moved forward and spoke in a defiant tone.

"I mean our green friends here old man. They are strange indeed I think!"

"How do you know they're green? Can you see through their hoods?"

"I feel their presence," he replied.

"Well, we're no friends of yours!" Fern rebuked.

"That's a great shame," the odd fellow answered. "I may be able to help you."

"How could you possibly help us?" Hickory was filled with mistrust.

"I can get you into the castle," his eyes sparkled with delight.

"That castle could not be taken by a thousand men-at-arms with siege towers, trebuchets and catapults," Nathaniel retorted.

"So how can you help?" asked Hickory warily.

"I am a singer of songs, a teller of tales and a maker of music," the man smiled back at him. "Some call me a troubador, a balladeer, a minstrel even, and tomorrow night, I play for the constable himself."

The children watched Nathaniel stroke his chin, in a now familiar fashion, as he considered this proposal of help. Then, the old man turned to them and whispered, "He may be our only hope. We haven't found anybody else who can help us and we cannot get inside the castle by ourselves."

The children reluctantly nodded their agreement and turned back to face the stranger.

"What's your name?" Fern inquired.

"Now, that's a very good question young lady."

"Well then give me a good answer!" Fern snapped back.

"In the courts of France I am known as Pascal the Player, in Venice they called me 'la Galisso', the Lark, and in Burgundy I am Piers the Poet."

"You have many names," Nathaniel stated. "Which one can we trust, I wonder?"

"Many different names for many different faces old man!" the troubadour replied. "And you are right. Not all of them are to be trusted, but you may call me Harlequin. That name you can trust."

"I still don't understand how you can get us into the castle," Fern interrupted. "We do stand out a little, in case you hadn't noticed."

"Oh I have noticed alright! But sometimes it's good to stand out from the crowd. Meet me here at sunset tomorrow evening and all will be revealed."

Suddenly, footsteps echoed on the cobbles and Nathaniel and the children turned to see who was there. It was an angry fisherman returning to seek recompense for his lost coins, but when they turned back to Harlequin . . . he had vanished!

30: The Whalebone Inn

~ Idle gossip and careless chatter, is often of things that do not matter ~

They spent an uncomfortable night trying to sleep under an upturned fishing boat on the shore and were woken early by the noises of the harbour. Voices cried out on the wind whilst sails were unfurled and anchors were drawn up, as the fishing fleets set out. In the distance, market traders and stallholders sang out as they advertised their wares. And echoing all this in the background, were the seagulls, who cried out overhead and then swooped to the shore to squabble over breakfast.

But there was no breakfast to be had for the three strangers hiding under the boat. "We can't sit here 'til evening," Nathaniel spoke with a tired voice as he rose from his sandy bed.

"Where are you going?" Hickory asked.

"Into town to bring back some food," he replied. "I also know the best place for news in a town like this. So you two stay here and I'll be back as soon as I can." With that the old man slipped under the side of the vessel and was gone. The two green children sat back in the shadow of the boat and waited.

"These are strange times indeed what with that there wild man of the sea and the rumour of these green children." It was lunchtime in a packed and bustling Whalebone Inn and a gruff voice coughed out the words in front of the fireplace as a crowd sat down to gossip in the centre of the inn.

"Now I hear of a great black dog up in Norfolk eating sheep and babies. The scourge of the countryside," the old man who held centre stage continued talking as he took his ale and sat on the three-legged stool by the fire.

"And I met a man from the fens who tells of a great worm that appears and devours villagers." A ruddy-faced sailor now spoke up and took on the theme of the conversation.

Nearby, another old man sat hunched in the far corner of the inn stroking his white beard in thought. He reached forward for his tankard of ale; the warm beer tasted good and he sipped gratefully at the brew. He was shrouded in smoke from the fireside and his hooded cloak obscured his face from the general throng but as the conversation grew more interesting he pulled down his hood and bent in towards the crowd to listen.

"Then there's that outlaw up north who hides in the woods around Nottingham," the sailor continued.

"Aye," replied the old storyteller, "the Wolf's Head. He that defies the local sheriff. Now what's his name?"

But no answer came, for the inn door was suddenly flung wide open and a young lad pushed his way into the tavern. As the voices of the customers fell away the boy exclaimed loudly, "He's in the harbour! The wild man is swimming in the harbour!" Within moments the inn was empty, as locals and sailors alike, spilled outside into the street and ran to the harbour-side to see the wild man.

Back under the hull of the boat, the children were dozing when they were alarmed by the voices of a crowd, over the sandbank, between them and the quay. As they listened intently to the cries a boy's voice rose above the others and as his words reached the boat the children looked into each other's eyes and smiled knowingly. Hurriedly, they stood up and without saying a word they slipped out into the sea-misty sunshine.

Not far from their resting place the constable of the castle looked down into the grey waters of Orford harbour and watched with interest as the wild man appeared from beneath the waves and splashed with glee. But

Bartholomew de Glanville had not given the creature his freedom. He only wanted to see how the beast behaved in the water and he had allowed the creature to swim only within the great nets that the castle guards now held all around the harbour wall.

While the wild man enjoyed his brief moment of freedom, the children deftly criss-crossed the dunes and made their way towards the shingle bank that ran up against the stone bulwark of the harbour. Then they lay upon the ground and edged their way slowly up the bank to try and see him. The pebbles were rough against their chests but they endured their pain. They had to see the green man below them and a longing desperation rose within them as their father's face burnt into their eyes. At last, as the sun broke through the early morning mists and glistened on the waves, they reached the top of the bank and carefully, anxiously, they peered over the harbour wall.

And the man they saw was indeed green but as his face turned towards them, their hearts sank like stones thrown into the sea, for he wasn't their father!

All their hopes lay crushed. Their long journey now seemed wasted and for the first time in many days they felt lost and alone once again. Fern moved towards her brother as he wiped a salty tear from his cheek and she clasped him close.

They looked desolately back upon the creature swimming in the dark waters below and found that they could not take their eyes from him. He was green, but he was covered in hair. His beard was unkempt and his eyes were as wild as the sea from whence he came. As the guards closed upon him and forced him out of the water and up the stone steps of the harbour wall, the jostling crowd jeered as they watched the wild man's ascent.

The constable stepped forward and looked down upon him as the guards manacled his feet once more. "Take the heathen beast back to the castle dungeon and keep him shackled," de Glanville bellowed. The wild man yelled out in pain as the two royal soldiers pulled at the chain around his neck and as it sprang taut the creature was jerked upwards and on to his feet.

Watching from afar, the green children also felt that pain. They felt his sorrow, his fear and his loneliness too and they realised that they couldn't leave this fellow creature of the wilds to suffer any more. Somehow, they would release him!

Clumsily, the guards dragged their strange prisoner past the watching mob, over the cobbled stones of the square, through the wild grasses of the dunes and up the muddy track to the imposing darkness of the castle.

Then, as if the sea was trying to reclaim one of her own kin, a violent wind lashed at the soldiers, a rough squall arose from the harbour and spat sand in their eyes and a cruel salty sea air coiled around them like a snake. But the guards pulled their prisoner through the battling elements and they fought their way through the gale, passed under the outer gatehouse and up the stone steps of the great keep.

At the top of the narrow flight, the wild man turned away from his captors and gazed out to the murky sea. His piercing eyes searched the waves longingly. Deep within the well of his pupils, waves danced and gulls soared high. A melancholy haze passed over his face and then with a violent shove he was pushed back into the shadows of the stone keep.

31: The King's Castle

~ Cold men live in houses made of stone ~

"I have something terrible to tell you." Nathaniel spoke hurriedly, as he slipped back under the hull to find the children.

"The wild man's not our father!" Hickory finished the old man's sentence for him.

"But how do you know?" Nathaniel's face looked astonished.

"We were at the harbour. We saw him," Fern answered.

"Then there is no need for us to remain here any longer. We must leave Orford immediately." The old man bent down to pick up his knapsack.

"No!" Fern exclaimed loudly. "We cannot leave without releasing him."

"You don't mean to carry on with this do you?" Nathaniel's patience was waning.

"Did you look into his eyes Nathaniel? There is so much sorrow there. He is chained, shackled and lost in an alien world." She paused for a moment and her eyes welled up with tears as she glanced across at her brother. Then she looked deep into the old man's heart and softly said, "And so are we."

"I understand how you feel about this," Nathaniel replied, "but we can do nothing for him! You saw how well he is guarded."

"We can still help him," Hickory now spoke up. "Harlequin will aid us."

"Don't be too sure of that one boy. He is as slippery as an eel. You know what a harlequin is don't you, he plays tricks on people, the word comes from the old French word Hellequin and that means a demon! I wouldn't be at all surprised if he betrayed us and delivered us all to the constable himself."

"I don't think so," Fern interrupted. "He will get us into the castle. I feel it somehow."

"You still wish to enter the castle?" Nathaniel's voice was incredulous but even as he spoke he saw the determined looks on their faces and knew that with or without him they meant to carry on. He then remembered Sir Richard's story about how the Abbot's rabbits had been released and he gave up his fight.

"Well, we had better get on with it then." The children broke out into smiles. "We'll lie low until dusk and then meet up with Harlequin. There's no time to waste. It must be tonight if you are certain you want to continue."

"Why must it be tonight?" Hickory inquired.

"Because tomorrow, all hell will break loose in the town because in the morning, the constable of Orford Castle plans to execute your wild man!"

"I think we should burn him!" A gaunt, pallid face spoke from the shadows of the constable's chamber. "That will smoke them out," and Silas of Wickham laughed at his pun. Yet even as Wickham laughed, he shuddered at the thought of burning flesh. And instinctively he put his fingers to the mess of black tissue that was once his left ear and winced at the recent memory of his escape from Rendel's forest.

The man he was speaking to finished putting his seal on a parchment scroll and wiped wax from his signet ring. Then he stood up from his desk and strode across the room to stoke the fire. "I am not overly interested in your elusive green witches Wickham," Bartholomew de Glanville replied curtly. "I want you to get rid of this wild man first."

"Yes, and I will my Lord," the witchfinder stepped into the torchlight. "But I can use him to my advantage. He will be the bait for my trap. These dratted green children believe he might be their father."

"But surely he is no kin of theirs," de Glanville looked up with interest as he warmed himself in front of the leaping, golden flames.

"Perhaps not, but I am certain that they will try to see him. Then, if we are vigilant, we will have them and the old man," Wickham crowed. "And then you will need plenty of logs, my Lord de Glanville," the witchfinder picked up a stray piece of kindling, "for I intend burning the lot of them."

32: The Gates of Orford

~ Voices that beguile, make the slow-witted smile ~

Night was falling upon the busy port of Orford. A shimmering moon began to appear above the grey sea and bright stars appeared in the black sky like silver arrows. The inn was full; the streets were busy with strangers and the torches of the castle battlements glared down searchingly upon the town.

Harlequin was as good as his word and they found him waiting exactly where he said he would be. They didn't tell him that the wild, green man was not their father or that they still planned to set him free but somehow they were certain he knew.

It was not difficult to see what the troubadour had planned to get them inside the fortress, as on their arrival he produced three gaudily decorated animal masks from his baggage and handed them to Nathaniel and the children. "Well, you three are now my troupe of performers. These masks will hide your faces and we should have no trouble in getting into the castle," Harlequin grinned. "How you get out again is your problem!"

The children tried their masks on for size and burst out into laughter as they looked upon each other. Fern had been transformed into a purple pig and Hickory had become a smiling black rat.

"Come on now children," Nathaniel tried to restore a measure of seriousness to the proceedings, but it was hopeless and as he put on his red feathered chicken mask, the laughter only got louder. So it was a merry troupe of performers that made their way across the cobbled square and up the muddy track to the black silhouette of Orford Castle.

The great mouth of the curtain wall of Orford Castle stood firmly shut as the four entertainers approached it. Red and gold banners flew high upon the battlements and rippled in the sea breeze like the sails of a great stone ship. Harlequin stepped forward and knocked loudly upon the heavy wooden door. The tapping echoed oddly in the silent night and at once a face appeared from the arrow slit above them.

"Who are you?" A slow, heavy voice lumbered down from the guardroom.

"We are the constable's entertainment for tonight," Harlequin replied courteously. "We are expected." He spoke with authority, even arrogance and the dull-witted guard was about to let them in without any problem but then the

Captain of the Watch stepped down from the battlements and interrupted.

"Show me your pass then Troubadour." He addressed Harlequin directly and the minstrel smiled and began to root around in his baggage. He suddenly looked anxious and Nathaniel, hiding behind his chicken mask, began to doubt him again. But Harlequin looked back up at the two soldiers and somehow his voice seemed to change in the night air. "You don't need my pass," he stated firmly.

The Captain of the Watch lifted the visor of his helmet and stared down at Harlequin. Then his eyes examined Nathaniel and the children. They all froze, fearful they were about to be found out. They gripped hard upon their masks and prayed for his gaze to pass over them.

Then Harlequin spoke again. "You don't need my pass," he repeated the words and his voice grew even stranger. It was beguiling, spellbinding, snake-like and the dull-witted guard was totally ensnared. "We don't need a pass, Sir." He spoke in a monotone to the captain but the captain had not yet been beguiled.

At that moment a soft voice called down to the officer from the keep and he turned to listen. "Let them through, the constable is waiting," the voice was barely audible but the captain immediately followed the instructions. The gate creaked open and the four entertainers marched through and the dull-witted guard led them up to the keep.

"That was fortunate," Nathaniel whispered to the children as they followed the mail-clad soldier.

"Yes," replied Fern, "and, how very odd that the voice from the tower sounded just like Harlequin's."

Nathaniel and the children stared at the troubadour but he simply smiled back enigmatically.

"Well, we're in aren't we!" he said, and then he broke out into song as he skipped merrily behind the lumbering guard.

❦

The night sky had turned a deep and endless black by the time the children walked carefully up the narrow stone steps that led to the first floor entrance of the castle keep. As they trailed the guard who now took them past the sentry, Harlequin passed a small bundle to Nathaniel. Whilst they talked merrily as they entered the door and went under the great iron portcullis, the children were more reluctant to pass into the keep. It was as if they felt that once they were inside, they might never come out again! They closed their eyes as they blindly took the final two steps and then the grill came down heavily behind them and they were sealed within.

When they opened their eyes again they found themselves in a small chamber that was brightly lit by torches and by the moonlight that filtered in through the arrow slits. To their right a flight of spiral stairs led downwards to the dungeon but they were taken left, through a large door and into another room.

It was the great kitchen and it was in utter chaos! Nathaniel and the children felt as if they had entered through the gates of hell itself. Flames burst forth from two great hearths, cooks shouted and swore, sweating spitboys turned huge boars amid great clouds of black smoke and a muddle of servants ran this way and that, carrying dishes of all kind.

Nathaniel licked his lips as a great haunch of venison was carried temptingly past him but the children just gasped at the sight of all the roasting meat that surrounded them. And when a baked peacock with all its feathers neatly fanned out behind it was taken past Fern on a wooden platter, she nearly fainted.

By now the dull-witted guard had returned to his post and it was Harlequin who quickly led them through this throng. He strode ahead as if he knew exactly where to go, though he had never played at Orford before. He turned and twisted around a scurrying maid with a fruit bowl and his hands coiled and uncoiled around her so quickly that only Hickory saw him grab two peaches from her saucer. He tossed them back to the children who hungrily bit into them as he now sipped beer from a tankard that he had swiped from another servant, and then he led them out of the mayhem.

"Well, as promised I have got you inside the castle." Harlequin spoke in a hushed tone as they stood in silence at the bottom of a flight of spiral stairs. "Now you must follow your path," he pointed at a narrow opening in the far wall, "while I entertain the constable and his guests."

Harlequin gave the children a wink, "Until the next time!" he grinned, and then he shook Nathaniel's hand and swiftly jinked up the stairs towards the Great Hall. With a quick wave of the hand he opened the door and danced inside and they never saw him again. Within minutes they heard the gentle singing of songs and the echo of laughter. Harlequin had been as good as his word and now they had to get on with their own task.

33: Out of The Depths

~ In dark places, you find sad faces ~

They guessed correctly that the opening Harlequin had pointed to was a back entrance to the dungeon and as they listened at the top of the steps they could hear the voices of two guards and the rattle of keys below them. Quietly they edged down the stairs into the darkness. Then, as they turned around the twisting steps they came upon the glowing light of the torches that lit the dungeon. The voices of the guards were louder now and in the background they heard another voice, though no words were discernible, just the tormented cries of a creature in despair.

Hickory took up the lead and as he went a step closer to the voices he found himself upon the bottom stair. He peered around the corner and saw the two guards throwing rotting fish at the beast that cowered behind the iron bars at the back of the cell. Anger and frustration tore through Hickory's soul, he wished he was grown to manhood and had a bright, sharp sword in his belt. But he had not and as he turned back to Fern and Nathaniel he didn't know what to do next.

But Nathaniel did, and now he unrolled the bundle that Harlequin had given him on their entrance to the keep. In the dim light Fern and Hickory did not at first recognise what the old man had but then he unfolded the material, took off his mask and put the cloth over his head. He passed his arms through it and there he stood in a royal crimson surcoat looking just like an elder member of the Royal Guard.

"I think he stole it from the guardroom as we passed through," Nathaniel's words met with the children's enquiring eyes. "Let's hope it will do the trick." Then the old man grabbed the two children by the scruffs of their necks and marched them down to the dungeon.

The children realised the old man's scheme immediately and played the part of downtrodden prisoners well. They kept their masks on so as not to alarm the guards too much and within seconds they entered the dungeon, much to the surprise of the two sentries.

"This pair are for the cells!" Nathaniel's voice was suddenly hard and sharp.

"Who are they?" the first guard asked suspiciously.

"Come to that, who are you?" the second one asked him as he took hold of the pommel of his sword.

"I've just arrived from Haughley Castle," Nathaniel answered convincingly. "There is word that the French are planning to invade and the east coast is being garrisoned to the full."

The two guards looked at each other worriedly. Either they were questioning the old man's story or the prospect of war terrified them. Nathaniel prayed it was the latter. "These two little beggars had disguised themselves and were caught stealing from our baggage. I thought a night in the cells of Orford would do them good."

The first guard stared at them suspiciously. "I'm going up to see the Captain of the Watch to find out more," and he grabbed his sword from the table and strode up the wide stairs that led up to the entrance chamber. The other guard moved away from Nathaniel and his prisoners and stood with his back against the bars of the far prison cell eyeing them coldly.

Suddenly, without any warning at all, the beast within that cell moved like lightning. A shaggy, green arm slipped through the bars and a large webbed hand gripped hard around the throat of the guard like a great snake. It held him tight. The guard squealed and then his eyes closed in pain. Seconds later, unconscious, he dropped to the floor with a heavy thud.

Nathaniel bent down swiftly and removed the keys from the guard's belt and quickly unlocked the prison door. Inside the cell, a leathery, green hand gripped upon the hard, iron of the cell bars and slowly the door swung open.

A webbed foot stepped out tentatively and then another joined it as the creature emerged from the shadows. Nathaniel stepped away from the wild man as he moved into the room but Fern and Hickory walked forward to meet him and as he came out from the darkness, his sea-grey eyes blinked in the torchlight. He stopped still and raised a long, hairy arm to cast a shadow over his face. Then, he turned towards the children and, through the half-light, he smiled at them, licked his lips and tasted freedom!

But at present, he was only free from his cell and not yet from the castle itself. "Quickly," Nathaniel whispered with urgency, "we must move fast." They all hurriedly turned away from the back entrance and made their way to the wider steps that led up to the small chamber by the front gate. They had to escape before the second guard returned.

❧

The moon shone brightly through the arrow slits of the tower and long white shafts of light danced on the spiral stairs as a hairy webbed foot edged out onto the bottom step. Two wild eyes peered around the corner and looked up to check the way was clear. Then the wild man, closely followed by Nathaniel and the children, quietly ascended the stone steps. A fierce wind blew in through the

shutters over the long window and the bolt
rattled and made the escapees jump with fear.
But then all was silent again.

As they reached the top stair they heard a
soft singing coming from the Great Hall above
them, and then the wild man sniffed the salty air
that blew in through the arrow slits and he smiled
with pleasure. But he was not out yet and before
them lay the great iron silhouette of the
portcullis. "The winch for this is in the chapel on
the next floor," Nathaniel spoke in a whisper as
he gripped the iron grill. "I studied a map of the
castle layout back at Wyken."

But the wild man did not understand what
was being said and he shook the portcullis with
rage. The clanging noise was too loud and Fern
ran to him and gently held his arms, then she
turned back to Nathaniel. "I will stay here with
him and stop him bringing the whole watch down
upon us. You go up and open it before the other
soldier returns."

She motioned the wild man into the
shadows of the entrance chamber and then
Hickory followed Nathaniel out of the room and
up yet more spiral stairs. As they approached the
chapel they could hear the gentle sound of
snoring. Luckily, whoever guarded the portcullis
winch was sound asleep. Hickory arched his body
around the corner of the door and peeped inside.

The grizzled face of the guard twitched in the half-light, the golden lion on his red surcoat rose and fell upon his chest as his heavy breathing echoed around the tiny chapel. Hickory tiptoed across the room to the winding gear of the portcullis and pulled as hard as he could but nothing moved, he could not budge it.

Below them, the wild man moved out of the darkness and tried in vain to push the iron grill upward but it was stuck fast. Nathaniel realised he had to help the lad so he slipped across to Hickory's side as quietly as he could and together they pulled hard upon the winch. Slowly, very slowly the teeth of the gears turned and from below they heard the jubilant groan of the wild man as he helped the portcullis on its way upward.

Nathaniel and Hickory continued to turn the gear but then the teeth of the chain caught and the mechanism clanked to a halt. The noise startled the guard and his voice muttered out. They stood rooted to the floor expecting the worst, but then realised the man was only talking in his sleep and they sighed with relief. They pulled again and the winch continued moving. Finally the portcullis was fully raised and below them the wild man unbolted the great door and flung open the doors to the black night.

Somewhere an owl hooted and the wind

sang out a nightime lament. The wild man felt the eternal pull of the ocean and Fern saw that need within him. She held his wrist and whispered gently in his ear, and then, without turning back, he ran out into the darkness. He rushed past the sleeping guards on the outer walls, slipped over the battlements and was lost amongst the dunes.

Inside, however, as Nathaniel and Hickory started down the stairs, the guard leant back too far in his chair and fell with a crash to the floor. The fall jarred him awake and then in the light of the torches upon the wall he saw the running shadows. With speed he grasped for the scabbard at his belt and clumsily pulled his sword out.

"Stop you devils!" the shout rocked the escapees and they halted briefly to look back at him. It was a mistake, within seconds the guard was upon them.

He raised his sword and caught Nathaniel a glancing blow across his shoulder. Nathaniel pushed Hickory against the wall of the stairs, pulled his own blade out, the one given to him by Old Winter, and turned to meet their pursuer.

It was an odd sight for in the flickering flames of the torches that lit the spiral staircase the thin aged frame of Nathaniel looked like that of a child faced with the onslaught of the burly guard who towered above him. But, what the old man lacked in speed and strength, he gained in experience and wisdom. His days as a crusader had left him with skill and cunning and he wielded his sword with a dexterity that belied his age. But the guard merely looked amused and then started to laugh at Nathaniel.

This was a fatal error, Nathaniel was raised to an unknown temper and as the guard made a lazy lunge at him expecting an easy victory, Nathaniel twisted his body out of the way and parried the guard's blade with ease. Before the soldier had time to realise what was happening, Nathaniel had plunged his sword up through the red surcoat, clean through the ringlets of the chain mail and into the soft flesh of the soldier's belly.

The guard screamed out in pain and grabbed despairingly at his wound. As he did so he dropped his own blade and it clattered loudly upon the stone floor. The guard's contorted face then turned to face the old warrior and he spat a Norman curse at his adversary before he fell headlong down the spiral staircase.

"Quick now, we must run before the rest of the watch is roused."

Hickory moved out of the shadows from where he had hidden during the duel and hugged the old man. "Don't worry about me, I'm stronger than I look," Nathaniel proudly stated.

As Fern climbed the stairs to meet them, the old man grimaced and bravely pushed out a smile, hiding the pain that now coursed through his right shoulder. "Come on then! Let's leave this place," Fern urged them on and Nathaniel and Hickory followed her down the steps and out into the moonlit night.

Just like the wild man, they too scaled the outer wall, and ran along the wall walk. Then the great bell in the guardroom at the top of the keep sounded the alarm and moments later shouts and cries echoed out from the towers of the castle. Luckily, the guards on the battlements looked out over the walls of the castle, expecting an attack from outside, and the three of them remained unseen.

As they approached the front wall, however, a brawny soldier turned back to look up to the keep and his gaze fell upon them. The man-at-arms shouted out for help as he unsheathed his sword and charged towards them. Hickory reacted first and grabbed a shield that lay up against the stone wall. He held it in front of him for protection and ran directly at the onrushing soldier.

Just before the moment of impact, however, Hickory closed his eyes and rolled to the floor. He winced with pain as his slight frame hit the hard stone but his trick worked for the soldier tripped

on the sprawling boy and was sent flying off the
battlements and screaming down onto the ground
below.

Nathaniel pulled Hickory to his feet and
brushed him down. "Just like camp-ball!" Hickory
said as he grinned at the old man.

All three of them now held hands and as the
soldiers swarmed over the battlements towards
them, they jumped off the castle wall and landed
softly in the dunes. A split second later, a green
hand appeared from nowhere and pulled them
into the swaying grasses and they vanished from
view . . .

"My Lord! He has escaped!" the thin voice
echoed timidly in the constable's chamber of
Orford Castle.

"Who, you fool?" Bartholomew de Glanville
sat comfortably in front of a raging fire, his
hounds at his feet, a goblet of wine in hand.

"The wild man of the sea," replied Simon
Gulliver, Captain of the Watch.

"How could this have happened in such a
great castle," another voice mockingly slipped out
from the dark recess of the room.

"It appears the guards were overthrown Sire,
one is dead and another badly wounded."

"Incompetents!" de Glanville sparked. The

knuckles of his hand turned white as his fury reached boiling point. "And who was in charge of the watch, Gulliver?"

"I was My Lord."

"Oh dear Gulliver! Then, it is you who must take responsibility," and in a split second of violence, de Glanville reached out for the poker by the fireside and crashed it down upon Gulliver's temple. The Captain of the Watch slumped to the ground in a crumpled heap.

As Gulliver lay there upon the hard stone floor he felt the coldness of the stone seep up through his whole body. A thin trail of blood trickled down from the wound and ran into his eyes blocking out his sight. His breath grew short and as he gasped loudly he heard de Glanville give a command to his dogs to finish him. Simon Gulliver clenched his fists and prayed it would soon be over.

From the shadows by the hearth, Silas of Wickham laughed out gleefully as the dogs played with Gulliver's dead body. However, his moment of delight was swiftly cut short.

"I'm glad you find this so amusing Silas," de Glanville rose from his chair.

"I'm sorry you have lost your pet," Wickham countered, "but I do find it entertaining to see a great fortress such as this, bested by a wild brute!"

"Well think about this Wickham. If the wild

man has escaped, then your bait has gone too and you have lost your chance to capture these green children - if such things exist!"

Wickham's face suddenly lost all colour as he realised de Glanville was right. "Damn them!" he barked.

Now, it was the constable's turn to laugh in amusement.

34: The Moon-Tide

*~ The sea and the moon live hand in hand and
one pulls the other across the sand ~*

"Where have you been?" Fern called out
from behind a sandbank.

"One last job," replied Nathaniel.
"Now there is a wild man carved on the font in
St. Bartholomew's church. That should please
the constable!"

Hickory grinned, he liked the way the old
man made faces out of the stone. One day he
wanted to try that himself.

For the rest of that night and all the
following day, Nathaniel and the children lay in
hiding amongst the great dunes that lay like
beached whales, between the land and the sea.
Cramped, hungry and cold they waited in a
silence that at times seemed to last forever. As
they felt the wind rise and fall and the rain
splatter down they knew that the season's change
was also bringing their quest here to an end but
what would that end be? For now, all around
them the vicious snarling of the dogs broke out as
the castle guards scoured the coastline, the woods
and the riverbanks.

And so they waited till the night came, until
the full moon rose and they could make their

escape. Only one route lay open to them now, only one route could evade the tightening grip that now seemed to clench all around them. For in a few more hours surely the patrolling pack of soldiers would enclose upon them and discover them.

A clear, luminescent white light shone down brightly upon the breaking waters of the North Sea. Huge waves crashed heavily upon the harbour walls of Orford and rocked the tiny fishing boats that lay anchored within. Larger vessels, trading ships from France and merchant craft from the east coast bumped into each other at their moorings as the moon-tide came into shore.

This was the moment the three fugitives had been waiting for. This was the sign to leave their hiding place, risk the chance of being seen and make their way swiftly down to the beach. Bands of torch-carrying guards and hunting dogs still roamed the area but as the night had fallen so their search had slowed down.

"It's now or never," Nathaniel shook the children awake as the full moon drifted behind a cluster of grey, autumnal cloud.

"I hope he's there," Fern shook sand from her cloak and fastened the clasp at her throat.

"So do I!" Nathaniel answered. "If he's not, then we've had it. On the beach, out in the open, we are bound to be caught!"

"He'll be there," Hickory rose up ready to move off. "Come on, let's go." He pulled his sister up and the old man followed them out into the open night and down to the shore.

As they ran they heard voices all around them but no-one followed and as they reached the beach they dived behind the cover of an outcrop of rock and gasped for breath. Hickory watched the waves closely. He was looking for something, and then as the moon lit up the shoreline he saw it. From the rolling waves a hand burst through the sea and waved towards him and he instinctively waved back.

All three of them scrambled out from behind the rocks and ran down to the beach. They stopped briefly to glance back at the black outline of the coast that stood behind them. The children thought of Till and Meg and of Sir Richard de Calne and then they thought of their missing father and they turned their gaze back to the sea. But Nathaniel's eyes lingered longer upon the shoreline.

"You do not have to come, Nathaniel," Fern met the old man's gaze. "You have helped us so much already."

"No lass, there's no going back for me now.

Wickham will have me burnt," Nathaniel smiled down upon them. "Besides, all this adventure's good for me!" And then calmly, he took Fern by one hand and Hickory by the other and they walked slowly out into the sea.

Waves lapped at their feet and then reached their waists and they shivered with the cold. Then suddenly from the murky depths three dark figures appeared before them. One of them they recognised immediately for it was the wild man of the sea. The other two were strikingly similar to him. Then they dived back under the waves and swam towards Nathaniel and the green children.

It was at this moment that a guard cursed as he lost his footing in the dunes and tumbled down onto the beach. As he rose he blinked as he saw the three fugitives walk out into the waves. As soon as he realised who they were he jumped to his feet and bellowed out through the moonlit night. "They are here, the witches are here!"

Within minutes the beach was swarming with red-cloaked soldiers and then two horses appeared on the sand. "It's them!" Silas of Wickham's shrill voice screamed through the air and he drove his black steed into the waves.

Bartholomew de Glanville, the Constable of Orford Castle himself, now tapped his spurs and followed suit. But the strong swell brought by the moon-tide fought back against the horses and as

223

Nathaniel and the children looked back to the shore they watched in awe as their hunters were halted by the crashing waves.

As Silas tried in vain to break through the thundering surf, de Glanville turned back to the shore and bellowed orders to his men. "Archers to the fore!"

A dozen or so red-cloaked men-at-arms ran into the lapping waves. Some of them carried great yew longbows; others immediately started cranking back crossbows and then de Glanville's shouts of command sung out again, "A reward for the man that hits his target. Now fire at will!"

A shower of arrows whistled in the still, night air and for a moment Nathaniel and the children held their breath expecting at any moment to feel the pain of the steel-tipped bolts striking them. But instead they heard only a whoosh as the arrows fell short of them and slipped harmlessly through the waves behind them.

With a renewed sense of urgency they strode out further but then the powerful tide washed over the children's heads and momentarily they struggled in the drowning depths. The three wild men rose from the sea and plucked the children from the swirling current. Then, Nathaniel, Fern and Hickory climbed upon the backs of the wild men and with a final glance back at the faces of anger on the shore, the wild men and their riders plunged out into the open sea.

Back on the beach the archers swore as they failed to win their prize and Bartholomew de Glanville looked for someone to blame for this latest mishap. The royal soldiers and their constable then turned away defeated and headed back to their castle.

One lone figure remained upon the beach. It was Silas of Wickham. He'd climbed down from his great horse, Minotaur, and stared coldly out into the sea. He listened to the cry of a lonely gull and felt the cold breath of the wind upon his burnt face and he fumed as the echo of merry laughter was carried back to him on the tide. And there upon that shore he swore a solemn oath that he would never rest until he had caught his green witches.

He took his long-bladed knife from its scabbard and the steel glinted in the moonlight. He ran the edge across his hand and winced as the blood rose from his palm. Letting a few drops fall to the sand, he climbed back upon Minotaur and rode away into the night.

As Nathaniel and the children slipped through the waves, they had already forgotten about the witchfinder. For now they were travelling north, up along the east coast of England, to find the forests of Barnsdale and

Sherwood. There they would look for another green man and hopefully this would be the children's father. But at present they knew him only through a name Nathaniel had overheard in the Whalebone Inn. A certain Robert of the Woods, although he was more commonly known as . . .

to be continued...

Historical Note

The legends of the Green Children of Woolpit and the Wild Man of Orford were both chronicled by William of Newburgh and Ralph of Coggeshall in th early thirteenth century. The tomb of King Rendel was inspired by a trip to Sutton Hoo and the burial ship of King Raedwald. The Bishop of Bury St. Edmunds really did have a summer residence in Elmswell and Sir Richard de Calne lived at a manor called Wikes, near Bardwell in Suffolk. The first constable of Orford Castle was called Bartholomew de Glanville and in medieval times it really was an impressive stronghold although now only the keep remains.

As for the Green Man carvings mentioned in the novel, well they really do exist and if you look carefully enough in and around the churches referred to, you can see them for yourself!

Woolpit - St. Mary's
Cotton - St. Andrew's
Walsham-le-Willows - St. Mary's
Tostock - St. Andrew's
Thurston - St. Peter's
Needham Market - St. John the Baptist
Grundisburgh - St. Mary's

Glossary

Azure - *the colour blue in heraldry*
Constable - *in charge of a castle when the Lord was away*
Demesne - *land belonging to the Lord*
Device - *design or emblem on a coat of arms*
Godsib - *godmother or godfather*
Harrier - *slender, narrow winged hawk*
Haywain - *cart that carried hay*
Hayward - *looked after the corn and hay*
Pennant - *flag*
Portcullis - *iron grill to protect the castle gateway*
Quintain - *a target used for practice with a lance on horseback*
Rebec - *medieval instrument like a violin*
Reeve - *official in charge of the Lord's farmland*
Shawm - *medieval instrument like a trumpet*
Solar - *Lord's private room*
Steward - *official in charge of the Lord's manor*
Surcoat - *tunic with coat-of–arms upon it*
Swineherd - *pig farmer*
Tithe - *Church tax*
Trebuchet - *a type of catapult*
Troubadour - *singer of songs*
Vassal - *person who holds land in return for services to a lord*
Villein - *peasant controlled by the Lord of the manor*
Yoke - *wooden beam to hold the oxen*

Bibliography

A Hedgerow Cookbook - *Glennie Kindred*

Food for Free - *Richard Mabey*

Suffolk Tales 1 - *Shirley Bignell*

Manors - *Edward Arnold*

Castles - *Edward Arnold*

Many a Good Horseman - *John Howson*

The Green Children - *Kevin Crossley-Holland*

Castles and Cathedrals - *David Aldred*

The Green Man - *William Anderson and Clive Hicks*

The Green Man in Britain - *Fran and Geoff Doel*

The Green Man - *Pitkin Guide*

Living in a Castle - *R. J. Unstead*

A Medieval Feast - *R. J. Mitchell*

Medieval Realms - *James Mason*

Presenting the Past - *Tony McAleavy, Andrew Wrenn, Keith Worrall*

Celtic Folklore Cooking - *Joanne Asala*

Life in a Medieval Castle - *Alison and Michael Bagenal*